HER

C.M. Serpell

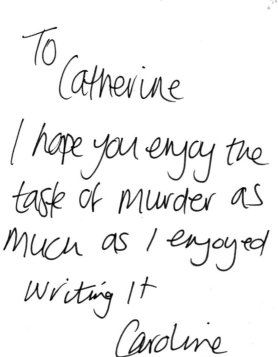

To Catherine

I hope you enjoy the
task of murder as
much as I enjoyed
writing it

Caroline

About the Author

C.M. Serpell lives in the South West of England with a small geriatric cat and an even smaller dog.

She spent most of her career working in a prison. Whilst there, she worked with men convicted of a wide range of offences. She worked in various roles from rehabilitation and substance misuse, to teaching business start-up and social enterprise. She has now hung up her keys and fulfilled a lifelong dream of writing her first novel.

First paperback edition May 2023
ISBN 978-1-7393659-3-6 (paperback)

Contact:
www.cmserpellauthor.co.uk
Instagram: @cmserpellauthor
Facebook: C.M. Serpell Author

Dedication

How do you choose who to dedicate your first book to? I don't think I can. You see, everyone in my life has helped me become the person I am today - the person who wrote this book. So, whether we met briefly, we speak every day, or somewhere in between - thank you for your part in my life.

This is for Everyone.

(Concerned you didn't make the Dedication Page by name? Check out the acknowledgements at the back – you might have better luck there!)

Marie

Marie froze at the car door slamming outside the house. She glanced at the clock - ten past nine - late enough that Carl would be drunk. Another crash – she flinched as the front door slammed. She waited in the dimly lit living room until Carl appeared in the doorway, his body silhouetted in the light from the hallway.

'Where are the kids?'

She noticed an edge to his tone and spoke carefully, not wanting to antagonise him. 'In bed. They have school tomorrow.'

'I know they have school tomorrow; they're my bloody kids. I told you to keep them up tonight. I wanted to put them to bed.'

Marie held in the urge to say that he should have come home after work instead of spending all their money at the pub, instead saying, 'They asked for you, wanted a bedtime story.' She always held in the urge to say what she thought these days.

'Are you calling me a bad parent? I go out to work all day to provide for this family, and you can't even make the effort to see I get to give them a kiss goodnight.' He staggered towards her, and she jumped up, slipping past him into the hallway, offering to put some food in for him.

'You think I want to eat that muck you call dinner?' Carl followed her into the kitchen, snatching the plate of leftovers out of her hands and throwing it into the sink. Red sauce created a lurid spatter pattern in the sink and up the tiles and the plate cracked. Marie could smell beer, smoke and stale sweat, his breath warm on her face. Her heel hit the skirting board as she stepped backwards. She bit her lip, focusing on the pain and tangy metal taste. Her heartbeat was loud in the room as Carl filled the space between them.

'Why are you backing away from me? Most wives would be glad to welcome their husband home, but not you, Marie. You think you are better than everyone else.'

She opened her mouth to protest and closed it again.

'What's the matter? Nothing to say for yourself? Too busy planning how to spend my money, I suppose.' She said nothing, and he slammed his hand against the wall behind her. Marie tried not to wince as he caught her hair.

He sneered at her, 'You're not worth it,' and turned away. Marie waited as she heard him go upstairs and close the bathroom door behind him before she let out a shaky breath. She wiped Carl's spit from her cheek, smoothed down her top, and went to clear up the broken plate. How was this her life now? This wasn't how she had planned it. This wasn't how life was supposed to be.

Carl

Carl clambered into bed, frowning, his shoulders hunched. He only intended to go to the pub for one drink after work with the lads, but then the fit barmaid was working. He enjoyed the banter and much preferred her company to Marie, who was never happy. This was all Marie's fault – if she weren't such a miserable cow, he wouldn't have to go to the pub to get some attention, someone who respected him and valued his company. Marie was trying to turn the kids against him, deliberately putting them to bed before he got home. She knew he wanted to see them. Tiredness and alcohol took over his thoughts as he closed his eyes and let the sleep take over.

Carl came downstairs in the morning and took the mug of coffee Marie silently handed him. Grumpy cow. He tried to remember what he saw in her. Back when they were at school, she always had that air of superiority, but her looks made up for it back then. She would get on the school bus two stops after him, shyly glancing towards him and his friends on the backseat before taking her usual seat towards the front of the bus with her sister. He remembered her in her school uniform and felt fresh annoyance at what she had become. Carl was once the envy of the other lads – he had the girlfriend with the biggest knockers, and now he was the one with the nagging wife whose saggy tits and miserable face were enough to put anyone off their dinner. Carl took a seat at the table with their twin daughters and helped himself to some pancakes from the stack Marie had made. Marie remained standing, occasionally leaning over the girls to help cut up their pancakes, chatting to them about school. The toot of a car horn signalled that Carl's friend John was outside to pick him up for work. He rose from the table and ruffled his daughter's hair before heading out of the door, shouting that he would be late home tonight.

As the taxi pulled up outside the house, the windows were in darkness. Carl paid the driver and stepped on to the garden path, the security light coming on and illuminating his short walk. He fumbled with his key in the lock, eventually dropping it. Exasperated, Carl knocked on the door. Where was she? He became more impatient, his knocking turning into a hammering, shouting for Marie to let him in. He didn't notice the neighbour's light come on. His own hallway light came on eventually, and he saw Marie's silhouette coming towards the door. He stumbled into the hallway as she opened it and looked at her. She was in a state, standing there in her old dressing gown, bleary-eyed. She closed the door behind him, pulling her dressing gown around her and retying the belt, then turned to go up the stairs.

'Nothing to say for yourself?' He noticed her stop, her shoulders stiffening as he asked the question. He spoke again, 'Not going to apologise?' She turned slowly, looked at him, then turned back to continue up the stairs. 'I asked you a question,' he spat.

Marie turned again and said, 'Please, Carl, not tonight. The kids are asleep.' She had that pathetic, pleading look in her eyes. He worked hard to provide for the family, and she didn't even bother waiting until he was home. He hadn't registered that it was 2 am – it didn't matter to Carl what time it was; it was the principle of it. She should wait for him, the man of the house. He lurched forward, his hand shooting out, grabbing a handful of her hair before she had a chance to give it a second thought.

He pulled her towards him and said in her ear, 'I think sorry is the word you are looking for.'

She whispered, 'sorry.'

'I didn't hear you. What did you say?'

'Sorry,' she said, louder this time.

He threw her to the floor, the lamp on the hall table clattering to the floor as she fell against it. 'You clumsy bitch, now look what you've done. I suppose I'll be expected to work overtime to replace that.' He looked down at her. Her dressing gown had fallen open, and she wore that awful nightdress she insisted on wearing. Other wives wore nice underwear and silky nighties, but not his wife. He had seen a glimpse of his barmaid's bra when she leaned over earlier. That was more like it; he smirked at the memory of the lace against her young pert breasts. Marie was crying now. He felt nothing but disdain for her. As she went to get up, he drew his foot back and kicked her in the stomach. Winded, she fell back again, knocking their wedding photo off the wall. He saw their smiling faces under the shattered glass, watching her hand reach out to pick it up. He stamped his foot down on her hand, moving the heel of his work boot around, grinding her hand into the broken glass. She cried out, and when he moved his foot, he saw her bloodied hand where the glass had cut into her flesh.

'Look at the mess. You're pathetic,' he shouted as he picked up her by her hair and aimed his fist towards her face, feeling her teeth scrape against his knuckles as he made contact.

Marie stifled her cries as she heard the word, 'Daddy?'

'Go back to bed, Darling, Mummy fell over, and Daddy is just helping me up.' The little footsteps quickly retreated along

11

the landing, and Carl threw his wife to the floor as he heard a siren approaching.

The Professionals

Tom had seen it all in his years on the force. Another day, another domestic call out. This was not the first night he had been called out to Carl and Marie's, and he felt sure it would not be the last. When would these women learn? When would they stop being such doormats, taking whatever abuse their significant others would throw at them? The police were called, and when they got there, she would say nothing was wrong, or she fell, and she refused to press charges. It was always the same old story where the women insisted; they were loved, and he didn't mean it. They spent time in the cells or a short sentence on remand and then went back to carry on. Nothing ever changed. Even if they bothered to attend their appointments at probation, they just went through the motions. Tom thought back over the past few days where, yet again, Carl was back out on the streets, free to return home. There was so much support out there for women in abusive relationships; Tom always tried to refer them to Revive. Revive was a local women's project that provided counselling services, support groups and help for women in abusive relationships. Despite the referrals and support he offered, he knew most of them were too blind or too scared to accept the help. It was hard when there were children, and they had to involve social services. Trouble was, even prison wasn't much of a deterrent these days. It wasn't the nicest place, granted, but they were all single cells now at the local jails. Prisoners had too many human rights these days, sitting in their cells with PlayStations, drugs and phones there were smuggled in. At least at the weekend he could enjoy a night out with friends and colleagues and forget about work. Tom thought of himself as one of the good guys.

~

Saturday night rolled around quickly, and work nights out always followed a similar pattern. They would start at a bar on The Barbican until everyone arrived, although they never really knew who would turn up once word-of-mouth spread. Some came for a couple of polite drinks, and others ended up dancing on the tables in a local dive bar until the sun began to rise. Tom enjoyed seeing his female colleagues out of uniform and letting their hair down.

The night promised to be a good one as the probation staff were coming out, as well as some girls from Social Services. Some of them came across as uptight, but Tom knew once they got a few drinks inside them, they'd loosen up. He just needed to get a few rounds of shots on the go. Tom smiled as he saw Emma, working her way through the bar in his direction. She and her friends looked stunning, with curves on display in all the right places. He recognised one of them, Beth, but the other one must have been new. Emma had her hair down, with curls flowing in front of her shoulders, nicely framing her cleavage in a low-cut top. The summer had been good so far, and her skin was bronzed and glowing. She looked good, and she knew it. This made her even more

14

attractive to him. She shot a cheeky smile in his direction and then diverted towards the bar. More people were arriving now, and Tom was sure this was would be a good night.

Carl

Carl had popped out to get a takeaway. He knew he had to be on best behaviour – Marie and that uptight bitch from probation were acting like best friends, plotting against him, setting him up to fail. He was lucky he hadn't faced another stay at HMP Exeter this time, but Marie was too pathetic to say much when the police questioned her. He had been released pending further investigation, not that he had much to go home to. Marie looked even worse than usual, and he really didn't want to return home with her grotesque face swollen and bruised. She didn't even try to make any effort to cover it up and look nice for him. Why did she always have to antagonise him? They had a meeting with the Social Worker tomorrow. She was another one who always thought she knew better than everyone else and was always trying to get Marie to take his children away from him. They all had another thing coming if they thought he would let that happen. Dumb bitches, let them try.

Marie was already trying to turn his girls against him. When he got home from the police station and called them over to him for a hug, they both stayed by their mum's side, looking up at her for approval before they tentatively came to him. It hadn't occurred to him he was not looking his best either after a night in the cells, and this was probably scary to them, especially after seeing their mum and dad fighting and the police turning up. At least Carl had read them a bedtime story while Marie tidied up their toys downstairs. You would have thought she would have tidied up before he got home, but he had held his tongue. Best behaviour.

It was the weekend, and The Barbican was getting busy. The smokers were gathering outside the pubs, getting louder as they got drunker. The bars were pumping out music to entice passers-by, and the takeaways were busy. The air had that friendly aroma of a warm summer evening. It was the perfect night to round up some lads and have a few beers, but he would have to wait a couple of weeks before he could get away with that. Carl decided to make the most of the opportunity of being away from his wife's judgemental looks and get a quick drink while waiting for the takeaway. He could always blame them if he was a little longer than Marie expected. The pub was busy, but not uncomfortably. He found a seat at the bar where he could chat to the young girl serving. The first whiskey slid down easily, immediately relaxing him. He ordered a pint so he could enjoy it slowly whilst admiring the view behind the bar. She clearly loved the attention, or she wouldn't have worn the push-up bra and skin-tight jeans. As she bent over to put the glasses away, he glimpsed her thong poking out the top of her jeans. He leered appreciatively. He would have a cigarette and maybe one more at the bar before collecting the food.

Her

Carl was well known to her, with his recent arrest being only a few days ago. From her position in the bar opposite, she watched him come out of the pub and sit at a table with a pint. He drained it in two long gulps, and the barmaid appeared almost immediately, bringing another pint and a small glass with a golden liquid in it. *Whisky?* The barmaid laughed at something he had said, her smile not quite reaching her eyes. Carl's eyes followed her as she walked away. *When will these men learn? When will they stop making the same mistakes? Getting drunk and leering over women? A few days since his arrest, and here he is in the pub, drinking again.*

She laughed at something someone in their group said, not paying attention. She watched Carl down his drinks and stand in the small queue outside the takeaway next door. Darkness was falling, and he glanced at his watch. She watched as he left the chip shop, holding his bag of food and heading along The Barbican, his back to her now. She peeled away from the group muttering something about stepping outside for some fresh air, and darted through the back lane, almost parallel to the main street Carl was taking. She didn't know why she was following him. There was no plan. Her heart was racing; the back lane was a steep incline, shadows all around. There was no one else around, and the lack of street lights made her skin prickle. She stopped and listened to the noise from the bars nearby. Occasional shouts and shrieks echoed off the water in the harbour, making it hard to judge how far away the music and sounds were. Just ahead, she saw the top of the steps that would bring Carl face to face with her, illuminated in the one streetlight. She heard footsteps on the cobbled steps, a slight rustle of a carrier bag followed by the sound of a zip. *Great,* she thought. He had stopped to relieve himself in the alleyway. She hardly dared to breathe as the splashing of liquid on the steps stopped and was replaced by his zipper and the click of a lighter. Her heartbeat quickened again, and she wrinkled her nose as cigarette smoke wafted up the steps heralding his arrival. When he was a few steps away, she turned the corner and stood in front of him. She saw a fleeting moment of recognition in his eyes before they widened, his mouth opening wordlessly as he fell backwards. His bag and cigarette dropped to the floor as his arms failed to reach the old iron railing. The crack as his head hit the stone echoed in the old stone stairwell, his body at an unnatural angle. She paused, looking over his body, expecting feelings of remorse. *Surely you should feel some sort of guilt after killing a man?* Her face flushed, her shining eyes glinted in the streetlight, a slow smile spreading across her face.

Her racing heart settled as the feeling of accomplishment washed over her. Her stomach rumbled at the salty aroma from the fish and chips. *No point letting them go to waste.* She picked up the bag and strolled back down the alleyway to re-join her friends.

'Anyone want a chip?' she offered.

The Professionals

Tom had around four hours sleep, and was simultaneously fighting his nausea and nursing a headache. He poured a handful of tic-tacs into his mouth to mask the smell of stale alcohol and leaned his face against the cool glass of the car window.

'You look like shit, mate,' Phil observed. 'Looks like I left at the right time last night. I'm too old for that these days. I like my two pints, then home to the missus'. The car sped out of the station towards The Barbican, Phil switching on the blue lights and siren.

A member of the public had been walking her dog when she found a body.

Phil and Tom arrived at the same time as the ambulance and nodded in acknowledgement as they all made their way to the alley.

The Barbican was quiet before the hustle and bustle of the day. Some bars had cleaning staff in, and Tom heard the muted clinking of bottles they restocked. In a couple of hours, the breakfast crowd would arrive, closely followed by tourists and families looking for a day out. The quirky cobbled streets and Elizabethan architecture housing restaurants and shops attracted a diverse crowd. A recent addition to the area was the merry-go-round by the harbour, near where they had pulled up.

The alleyway, where the body was found, was a steep set of steps that connected the main road of The Barbican with the back streets. Two women sitting on the pavement near the bottom of the steps identified themselves as making the 999 call. Tom asked them to wait whilst he and Phil accompanied the Medics to the body. The dim alleyway was soaked in the stench of damp and urine. One medic passed Tom the dead man's wallet. He noted the usual array of bank cards, Tesco Clubcard, dentist appointment card, a family photo, and some receipts. Tom flicked through the receipts noticing a large order for fish and chips the night before. He surveyed the scene before him and saw none, then glanced overhead at the circling seagulls and shrugged, thinking the gulls must have eaten them. After looking at the man's face, he pulled out the family photo and recognised Carl. He had been in the cells on more than one occasion for beating his wife, Marie. They had two little girls.

'It couldn't have happened to a nicer man,' Phil commented drily as he made the same connection.

Another two patrol cars arrived, quickly followed by a couple of Detectives.

'Looks like he fell,' Tom said as they strode towards him and Phil.

Katie had arrived in one of the patrol cars, and after a discussion around identification, she and Tom were tasked with visiting the wife.

Marie

They couldn't confirm that it was him, but the officers told her a body matching Carl's description had been found. Marie stared at them, her mouth dry, with no words coming out. Carl was her childhood sweetheart and the father of her children. A wave of nausea hit her, and she ran to the bathroom. She stood in a daze running her hands under the tap, and looked at the face staring back at her in the mirror. The bruises were changing colour each day, and there were grey bags under her eyes.

Marie made her way back to the living room, where the nice female officer had made her a cup of tea. She identified herself as Katie and gave her card to Marie to call anytime. Marie winced as she took a gulp of steaming tea. She heard her daughters' laughter drifting down the stairs.

'What am I going to tell the girls?' she asked Katie, her eyes wide.

'Is there someone we can call to come and support you?' Katie gently asked. Marie frowned. She didn't have many friends these days. Carl said she didn't need anyone else, and he should be enough for her. He didn't like other people poking their noses in his business. As Marie grabbed her phone from the hallway, the glassless wedding photo caught her eye, and she felt a dizzy rush of adrenaline - she was safe.

Her hand throbbed at the memory of the glass cutting her flesh, the bandage still wrapped around the wound as a reminder. A lump in her throat immediately followed her sense of relief and safety, her eyes filling with tears.

The Social Worker was due to visit later, and Marie asked Katie if she would cancel the visit. She couldn't deal with Beth and her questions today.

An hour later and it was just Marie and the girls again. Her sister was on the way from Bristol, and Katie was going to arrange formal identification of the body. Marie jumped as she heard a knock at the door. She looked out the window and saw Beth, the Social Worker, on the doorstep. Marie sighed and opened the door.

'I am so sorry for your loss. I still wanted to check in, in case there is anything I can do to support you, but we can reschedule today's assessment.' Beth left a card with her number and gave the same spiel as Katie about calling any time.

Marie stared at the card in her hands. She tore it in half and dropped it into the empty mug on the coffee table, sinking down into the sofa. The clock, a wedding anniversary gift, ticked loudly in the quiet room. The girls were silent upstairs. Marie took her phone out of her pocket and looked at the screen. *Should she call people and tell them about Carl yet?*

The Professionals

Emma smiled, feeling her heart swell at the thought of the weekend. The flirting between her and Tom hadn't gone unnoticed, and the girls in the office asked Emma for the details. She knew how to play the game, and she played it well. Tom was a man who liked the chase and liked to be kept on his toes. She stayed out late enough that he would not go home with anyone else but not late enough to get drunk and sleep with him. Tom was married, but he had confided in her that things were not going well. He would make a great stepdad to her little boy. She needed someone like Tom - stable yet ambitious, with a good salary. She pictured his cheeky smile and how his shirt stretched over his muscular chest. At least she could go out and have fun on the occasions her ex wanted to play doting dad.

Emma didn't give in to requests for gossip from the girls, smiling as she shrugged her shoulders, saying nothing. She opened TEAMS Messenger on her laptop to ask what her friend and colleague, Beth, was up to. Emma worked in the Adult Social Care department at Social Services, but her best friend, Beth, was in the Children's Team. Emma was hoping for a lunch date to catch up on each other's weekends. Beth had everything Emma wanted - husband, two children, a lovely house, even the perfectly behaved spaniel. Beth enjoyed hearing Emma's tales of dating and nights out. Emma saw the dots appear as Beth typed, *I have two families to visit following issues at the weekend, but yes to lunch after that.*

Emma's phone rang. It was the police asking if she was free to attend a Welfare Check with them on one of her cases. She sighed and grabbed her bag. The police didn't do many Welfare Checks these days, and Emma was lucky they were doing it at all, let alone keeping her in the loop.

During the drive there, Emma mulled over the possibilities of what she might find. She had been lucky so far in her career that she had found none of her clients dead. The client she was on the way to see was Fiona. Fiona was well known to many local professionals, though not disliked. She moved to Plymouth following a stint in rehab a few years ago and remained long after the rehab closed its doors for good. She had no family locally and wasn't in touch with her family in Leeds. Fiona described them as 'normal' and refused to talk about them beyond that. All she would say was that she couldn't bear for them to see what she had become, and it was better this way. Despite her somewhat sad, heroin-centred lifestyle, Fiona wasn't unhappy. In her own way, she accepted the life she had. This was often the case with the addicts who formed their community of people who no longer had a place in traditional society.

They had admitted Fiona to the hospital following an overdose more than once, not always accidentally. The hospital referred her to Social Services, where she was placed on Emma's caseload. She had been in a few abusive relationships with well-known individuals. Emma sighed, thinking about her; the girl didn't seem to learn from her mistakes, staying stuck in this cycle. She thought back to her many attempts to

25

get Fiona to engage with the local women's support project, Revive. Fiona refused. Emma even offered to drive her there, and Fiona wouldn't show up.

Emma pulled up outside Fiona's building at the same time the police car arrived. She recognised the two officers that got out of the car and nodded in acknowledgement. Emma blushed slightly, recognising one of them from the night out at the weekend, remembering her enthusiastic dancing and tipsy banter. The officer gave a friendly smile and wave and introduced herself as Katie.

As they approached the door to the building, a scruffy-looking boy came out. Emma estimated him at around ten, a similar age to her son. Her heart strings pulled at the thought of Ryan and his different life compared to this boy who probably never stood a chance. The boy pushed past, muttering 'pigs.' They caught the door before it closed behind him and made their way into the building, noses wrinkling at the stale smell in the corridor.

'Come on then,' the male officer said as he pulled on a pair of latex gloves, 'let's get on with this. The neighbour called it in. Said she hadn't seen Fiona in a few days. I don't know which is worse - nosy neighbours calling us all the time or us having to spend our days keeping these junkies alive.'

'Bit harsh, Phil,' Katie retorted sharply. Emma and Katie exchanged a look. Emma felt relief that Katie seemed to be one of the good guys; so many on the force had old-fashioned views like Phil that had no place in policing today. He was nice enough but clearly old school. Emma smirked at the image in her head of his 1950s views and lifestyle. His wife was probably waiting at home with his pipe, slippers, and a freshly baked pie. Her mind briefly drifted, wondering if Tom liked pie.

The door to the flat wasn't locked. They pushed it open, shouting 'Hello' and identifying themselves. Emma followed behind the officers who were ensuring the flat was safe, methodically checking the rooms whilst continuing to shout Fiona's name. It didn't take long.

'In here,' Katie shouted, as she found Fiona slumped on the floor at the end of the bed. Emma's heart sank as she took in the scene. Fiona's lips were tinged with blue, and there was a bit of red plastic wrapped around her arm as a tourniquet. There was a needle on the floor beside her. Emma noticed a bag for life on the bed with the handles ripped off. That explained the crude tourniquet. As Katie checked for a pulse, Phil used a gloved hand to pick up the needle, putting it on the bedside table.

'I've got a pulse,' Katie shouted, pressing her radio to request an ambulance despatch to them. Phil removed the tourniquet, and they carefully laid Fiona down in the recovery position. Emma let out the breath she hadn't realised she was holding. The paramedics arrived within a few minutes. Emma hung back until they drove away with Fiona.

Emma had given the paramedics her card. She would need to get an email out to everyone working with Fiona when she had an update from the hospital. As she pulled the handbrake on in the car park behind the office, her phone pinged with a Facebook notification. Katie had sent her a friend request. Emma saw 15 mutual friends and accepted the request, making a mental note to have a little creep of Katie's Facebook later.

Fiona

After a night in the hospital, Fiona was restless, her body craving heroin. She needed to get back out on the street to earn money. Her Social Worker, Emma, phoned first thing and was going to give Fiona a lift home from the hospital. Emma nagged Fiona, trying to get her to go to that women's counselling place again. She had also told Fiona's Probation Officer what had happened, so she would be nagging Fiona too. Fiona closed her eyes and lay back in the bed, she just wanted them all to leave her alone, but she knew she would have to play the game and say the right things to get Emma to leave once she dropped her home.

A few hours later, Fiona sank into the sofa as the drugs worked through her body. She felt the warm glow spreading through her veins, and the sofa was the softest, most amazing place to be at that moment. She smiled as she thought the sofa felt like sitting on a cloud. Fiona didn't notice the worn covers, speckled with burn marks, the slightly sticky finish and general appearance of squalor that surrounded her. All that mattered to Fiona at that moment was the heroin she had injected between her toes.

Fiona was pretty once upon a time, but now her cheekbones were sharp and angular, her hair lacklustre, and her skin dull. Despite this, Fiona didn't want to change. She wanted all the well-wishers to stop trying to make her. Fiona glanced at the table through the haze, eyeing the stash she had just scored. The handbag she had stolen earlier contained £150 and some jewellery she could sell later. Her stomach flipped with a brief pang of guilt as she remembered the face of the lady as she snatched the bag and ran. She pushed the feelings aside - the woman could afford it. Who walked around with that much cash and jewellery if they couldn't afford to lose it? It was probably insured anyway.

The next morning, Fiona woke up to her phone ringing. She squinted at the screen - 'Anna'. Her Probation Officer. Great. Fiona groggily swiped to answer the call and grunted. Anna reminded her about her appointment at the office in an hour. Fiona didn't mind Anna; she rang to remind her of appointments so she didn't end up breaching the terms of her probation. Although sometimes she still did. She would end up back in court, where the Judge usually just said don't do it again. Her last Probation Officer wasn't like Anna and appeared to enjoy it when she forgot her appointments, his eyes lighting up at the thought of sending her back to court. Anna was more understanding. Fiona liked her. She dropped the phone to the floor and went back to sleep.

Two hours later, Fiona made it to the Probation Office and explained to the receptionist that it wasn't her fault she was late as she had been in hospital. She crossed her fingers. Technically she had; it just wasn't today. She was told to have a seat. Ten minutes later, Fiona got the message; Anna was going to make her wait, and they would then have the same old chat about being on time for appointments, blah blah blah. She tried to settle into the uncomfortable chair in the waiting room, scrolling through Facebook, glancing up now and then when others came and went. A smart-looking man with a briefcase came in, and Fiona mused over what he could have done. He wore a formal shirt and black trousers, his beer belly and the veins on his nose telling her he liked to drink. He wasn't there long before an older man with a Probation ID badge came to the door summoning him for his appointment. Briefcase man had a name - Frank.

Anna eventually arrived at reception for Fiona's appointment. Fiona sat opposite her in the bare interview room, half listening while Anna gave her the telling off for being late.

'I am only saying it because I care. I just wish you would want to help yourself as much as those around you,' Anna said. Fiona had heard it all before; they were all pleasant enough and meant well, but everyone wanted to be the one who saved her, the one who inspired and motivated her to change her life. Fiona was supposed to attend a therapy course about addiction as part of her court-ordered probation requirements. She had gotten away without doing it so far. Anna said her time was up, and Fiona was enrolled to start next week at the local addiction agency, Phoenix. Fiona had been dragged along to various courses over the years. They were full of the same old faces. Even the people who convinced the staff that they were making a real go of it would usually be outside scoring afterwards. She attended Alcoholics Anonymous meetings for a while when she was serving a 3-month sentence at HMP Eastwood Park. That was only to get out of her cell in the evenings, or her 'room' as they insisted on calling it. She didn't know why they bothered. Call it what you want, it was still a cell or a cage. The people who ran the AA meetings always brought nice biscuits, so that was something.

Frank

No matter how hard Frank tried to stop drinking, he just couldn't. He wanted to stop, he really did, especially after what happened. Frank hadn't always been a drinker. He used to have a life. A family. A job. He enjoyed his job at the bank in the beginning. He started working there when he finished school as a cashier and worked his up to a role in wealth management. He met his ex-wife, Sonia, at the bank when she briefly worked as a cashier. They got married and bought the house and were so happy. He hadn't seen his mum that happy since before his dad passed away years before. It gave her a fresh zest for life. She loved telling friends about her successful son and his wife. Sonia got on well with his mum, and he couldn't have asked for a better wife. The house was always spotless, like something from a catalogue. The only trouble was she just kept spending money. Their bank account wasn't bottomless, and with every new pair of curtains or custom-made item of furniture, Frank felt the pressure building like an explosion in his head that he didn't know how to release. He wanted to mention the spending to her; he wanted to ask her to be mindful, but he didn't want to let her down. He was supposed to provide for her and give her the things that made her happy. He saw how her face lit up with pride and joy when she revealed each new purchase carefully placed in its position in their home.

Frank started opening a bottle of wine of an evening and suggesting they share it after work, but then she went on a diet, so he would drink the bottle alone. Alcohol helped to ease the pressure inside his head and relax his furrowed forehead after work. It stopped him from replaying the words of his manager, increasing targets and threatening job cuts. Alcohol stopped him from thinking about their dwindling bank balance and picturing the high price tags on the new furnishings she was buying. It stopped the tight feeling in his chest. When Frank woke up in the mornings, there were just the briefest of moments where he didn't remember the constant pressure, those fleeting moments before he opened his eyes bringing the feeling of impending doom. At work, his job was sales and target driven, and there always seemed to be younger, newer staff coming in who talked the talk better than he ever could. He hated going to people's houses and having to pressure them into investments and insurance. It didn't use to be like this; the job used to be about people, and now it was all about selling and badgering old ladies into handing over their life savings.

Frank began to have the odd drink at lunchtime to get him through the afternoon. Eventually, he was called in for a meeting with the Area Manager and told that clients and colleagues said he had been drinking during the workday. They were here to help, they said. He could talk to them if he had a problem, they said. What could they do? They couldn't stop Sonia's spending. They couldn't sit her down and have the conversation he was putting off about money, and they certainly couldn't match the warm glow that alcohol gave him. Frank felt the best way to deal with it all was to go to the pub instead of returning to his desk that afternoon. If Frank had known the chain of events that would come next, he would never have gone to the pub.

Every time Frank closed his eyes, he saw the girl bouncing off the windscreen. He remembered the strangest details - how some of her hair had caught in the wiper blade; it was blonde, her school bag at the side of the road, books spilling out of it where the zip had popped open. He remembered that her body was just out of his view when the police were speaking to him at the side of the road – and wanting to look to check she was okay, but the sick feeling in his gut stopped him from doing so. Frank remembered the breathalyser and hazy confusion at hearing the word 'girls' plural. He had only seen one. Frank didn't remember getting to the station or spending that night in a cell. He remembered nothing until the morning when he was told they would charge him with Causing Death by Drink Driving. It was then that he was told that both girls he had hit had passed away. Sonia said she couldn't live with the shame. She said she couldn't bear to come and visit him at the prison, and she wouldn't let that become her life. She said she would not let him drag her down with him. Sonia cried and said she wished he had spoken to her but that it was all too late now. He signed the divorce papers without a fuss, and they sold the house. She boxed up his belongings, and her brother took them to his mum's house to be stored in the garage. Frank's mum stood by him and visited him at the prison every week without fail. His face was in the papers. His mum was no longer welcome at her book club or local community events. She looked older and had aged ten years in the two years he was in prison. Frank was an only child.

On release from prison, Frank returned to Plymouth and moved in with his mum. He never saw Sonia again but heard she had already remarried. Frank's mum had changed her opinion and maintained that Sonia had never been good enough for her boy. Frank wanted to rebuild his life, but every day there were reminders of what he had done. His skin prickled, and his face flushed red at the looks he got from staff and customers in the local supermarket. They went for a Sunday Roast in their favourite restaurant and were asked to leave, told it was a family restaurant and they couldn't have people like him there, and that it would stop others from coming. His mum said nothing, but he could see the hurt. They never spoke about it, but she cooked a roast at home each week now. Frank could no longer work at the bank - not with his criminal record and drink problem. His Probation Officer said he needed to get better at managing his emotions without alcohol. They were making him do a course at Phoenix, the local drug and alcohol agency.

Frank looked around the room. The bright yellow walls were adorned with a mixture of posters – some motivational quotes and others giving information. There were a couple of large plants in the corner, and they set the chairs out in a circle. He looked at the surrounding people. People he would never have come across in his old life. He met these sorts of people in prison but tried to keep himself to himself. He had a good job in the prison as a Library Orderly and got little trouble. Frank completed some courses to enhance his CV, ready for release, though a few Customer Service and BICs courses didn't seem to win over any employers. Still, it gave him something to focus on.

This addiction course was another reminder of how his life had changed. He scurried into the building, hoping no one he knew would see him. It didn't occur to Frank how many people had seen him drunk or his face in the paper already. The course was twice a week for five months. Most of the others knew each other, and they eyed him and his formal style of dressing with suspicion. He recognised one girl from the probation waiting room. She introduced herself as Fiona.

The course was led by different professionals, including Anna and Grace from probation, a couple of police officers, staff from Phoenix and, he was told, a few other local organisations would offer some support. By coincidence, the police officer attending this evening arrested Frank when he had the accident. One of the staff from Phoenix was assigned as his key worker for the duration of the course, Kylie.

'I'm not here to Judge,' said Kylie. *They all judge*, thought Frank. She asked him to keep a diary of times he was tempted to drink. Every time he came to these meetings or courses, he wanted a drink. Every time he left, he had a drink. Sometimes he got home late, and his mum would be in bed. Other times she would wait up crying when she realised he was drunk again. He would squirm, his eyes darting around the room, anything but making eye contact. He didn't want to drink. Frank's drinking had all started to take away his feelings. He continued drinking to take away the shaking in his hands, to stop the sweating as he tried to resist. And now, since the accident, he needed drink more than ever.

The Professionals

Tom recognised most of the faces in the newest cohort for the addiction group. Fiona was a familiar face; he had more than his fair share of dealings with her over the years. Then there was the bloke he had arrested for drink driving, killing two young girls. It was a few years ago, but Tom would never forget the scene or the media coverage. To this day, there are always fresh flowers at the site of the crash. Tom remembered every detail like it was yesterday. Some cases stick with you more than others. There were a couple of working girls he had seen around. He didn't blame them for drinking or taking drugs to get through what they did every day. A young lad, Matt, was there following a fight in a pub when he was drunk – to be fair, he didn't seem to have much of a drink problem, more of an anger issue, but there was no anger course, so they didn't know what else to do with him.

Tom made a mental note to call Revive to see if they could send a member of staff to introduce their service to the women on the course at some point. He had the phone number of Sally, one of the younger members of staff there who had slipped it to him on a post-it when they were both attending the same training course recently. Tom smiled. He might ask her out for a drink when he called later. He liked Emma, the Social Worker, but she was clearly playing a game, and he wanted someone who would put out now. Since the baby, his wife wasn't interested in sex, always complaining she was tired or that he was only interested in one thing. *Yes, Sally would be a lovely way to spend his evening.* He sent his wife a quick text apologising that he had to work late before making the call to Sally. He knew she would accept; they always did. She giggled a lot on the phone, causing his jaw to clench, easing only at the thought of her tight little body.

After group, as Tom left the agency to head back to the station, he saw the usual suspects loitering outside. This was the perfect place for the dealers to wait. They caught the junkies in a vulnerable place, often craving as they had to remain clean for a drug test, perfect to approach as they left. There was a school opposite, and there were regular complaints from the parents, but short of stationing an officer there 24 hours a day, there was not a lot they could do. Resources were stretched at the best of times, and the public were never happy. They couldn't win. Gone were the days when anyone was grateful for the police force. Tom walked past the pub on the way back to the station and waved though the window at the group of probation staff he recognised at what looked like a leaving do for someone.

Katie was at her desk when Tom arrived back at the station.

'Katie, you gorgeous creature, how are you?'

'Just another day fighting crime and saving the world,' she grinned. Tom put a tray of Starbucks down on the table, gesturing for Katie to take the one nearest to her. She noticed his cup had a phone number on it with the words 'Call me' and raised an eyebrow at him.

'What? I can't help it if women find me irresistible.'

Katie rolled her eyes and began filling him in on events of the last couple of hours - a road rage incident and a budding brawl between two rival groups of teenagers in the city centre. The teenagers were dispersed, and the road rage perp was having some time out in cells before they would release her with no further action. As they chatted, the radio crackled, and Katie and her shift partner, Phil, were called out to a traffic collision.

'No rest for the wicked,' Tom said with a wink as she abandoned her Starbucks and strode out, keys in hand.

Her

When would these people learn? Day in, day out, they never changed. They had many opportunities to make things better, but no one ever took them. They all ended up back in the court, the same mistakes again and again. Each time, more people hurt along the way.

The wife beaters often had their faces splashed all over the front pages. Click bait headlines giving the impression of a juicy story at the expense of their victims' tattered dignity. The papers tell the atrocities of nuisance neighbours, drug dealers, and flashers, repeating the same vulgar acts. When would the world realise that trying to get them to change is futile - they never do. If society would not make people pay, something else would have to be done.

The addicts were the worst. Sewer rats, the lot of them - blame and selfishness, stealing from others to get what they wanted. She sometimes wished she could just put a dodgy batch of drugs out there and wipe the smack heads out en-masse. This would be too risky; she would be patient, play the long game, tread carefully and take them one at a time. She would wait and watch until the opportunity presented itself again.

She had been thinking about doing something about the state of society for a while; they all joked about it, but it was time to stop thinking and get on with it. Carl's death was opportunistic – an unexpected bit of luck. It felt serendipitous for him to be there on his own at the same time she was. *No-one else was going to clear up the streets and rid them of these miscreants. No, something needs to be done. Carl was just the beginning.*

Fiona

Fiona finally agreed to listen to what Sally, the counsellor from the women's project, had to say. Sally from Revive was another one who thought she could save every waif and stray. She clearly had a massive crush on the police officer helping to run the course and blushed every time he looked at her. Tom seemed a bit of knob to Fiona, too full of himself, but the poor deluded girl only had eyes for him. Fiona didn't have the best track record herself with men, so she could hardly blame Sally. The course was okay so far; she knew a few of the others and recognised Frank from probation. Fiona never turned to prostitution. That is where she drew the line, but she had nothing against those who did, so engaged in friendly introductions with the prostitutes in the room. The Phoenix staff were the same old mixture you always get at charitable agencies. They fall into a few categories – the young, fresh out of university staff filled with theories and ideals, wanting to change the world. They always thought they would be the one to save your soul and seemed to take it personally when you didn't give a shit. Sometimes this sense of purpose lingered longer term, but most became jaded middle-aged workers. The jaded middle-aged workers have been around a while and know most of the addicts by name, drug of choice and preferred crimes. This worker often gave up on the hope that anyone would change but stuck around because they didn't know what else they would do with their lives. Occasionally they would see a flicker of hope and be reminded why they got into this game, but the inevitable screw-ups came along, feeding the cynicism. The third type of addiction worker was the ex-addict, the reformed character. These guys were tedious. They love to spout their success stories alongside all the clichés – 'If I can do it, you too can find the strength'. Ugh. They still hung around addicts all day. They hadn't escaped that life. Whatever type of worker they were, Fiona was always polite and knew how to coast along under the radar without rocking the boat. This week her worker, Kylie, ('I'm not here to Judge,' Kylie), fresh-faced and ready to change the world, asked her to write a letter to herself from the future. She had to imagine ten years had passed, and she was writing a letter to tell herself what was different, what she had done to get to wherever she would be in ten years. Fiona did not know and couldn't really give a fuck, but she would find something to write. She knew they expected her to say she wanted to give up the gear. Fiona sighed. All these exercises were bullshit, but their eyes lit up when she wrote what they wanted her to.

It was fresher's week in Plymouth, and Fiona was getting ready to attend some house parties. She tapped her foot on the floor, causing her knee to shake as she applied her makeup, a shiver running down her bare spine in a backless halter top. Glancing around the room, her eyes came to rest on an empty methadone bottle. Fiona opened it, savouring the drops that ran down the side onto her tongue. The nights had become a ritual for her during fresher's week. She would totter around the streets near the university where the student houses and flats were, looking for the parties and just stroll in. These kids didn't know who most of the party guests were anyway - they had left the warm comfort blanket of their childhood homes and could party with no rules, no grownups. It was easy for Fiona to gate crash, with people often assuming she was an older sister or a mature student. The carefully applied makeup hid the tiredness that life had permanently etched on her face, the cleavage detracted from her angular limbs, and track marks were carefully kept to private areas.

Fiona pushed through the drunk teenagers, shouting greetings of familiarity and hugging people as she passed through downstairs, never lingering. She slipped up the stairs and made her way through the bedrooms. She never took much; odd bits of jewellery or cash lying around, enough that she could sell, but not enough that they would notice straight away. She pushed through the sweaty teenagers to the kitchen at the back of the house. Lots of the older houses in the student areas had a kitchen in the tenement on the back of the house with an exit to the rear service lane. Fiona scanned the littered worktop, selecting an almost full bottle of vodka for her next party – she hated turning up empty-handed

The Professionals

Kylie loved her job. She had recently graduated from university and was lucky to get a job as a Drug and Alcohol Addiction Worker at Phoenix. She worked closely with the women's project, Revive, and had a special interest in working with females. Kylie believed they all had it within them to give up the drugs and change their lives when given the right support and opportunities. She prided herself on never judging her clients and liked to tell them this regularly. Kylie would be horrified if she had to live next to any of them, but it was easy for her to shout about her lack of judgement from her nice, comfortable graduate life living in her parents' basement annexe.

'I know you prefer working with women, but it will be good for you to step outside your comfort zone.' Kylie's manager said as he passed her Frank's case file.

Kylie gave Frank her standard line, used with everyone - 'I don't judge. Everyone deserves the same chance to turn their life around.' She wasn't quite able to make eye contact with the man who had killed two young girls, shuffling her papers and clearing her throat. She couldn't understand how her colleagues didn't seem bothered by who they worked with.

Kylie didn't quite fit in with them yet. They were nice enough, but she was always on the side-lines, rarely directly included. Sometimes she would get invited to the nights out as an afterthought, but she would hear them planning it well before anyone thought to mention it to her. She heard a few of the girls planning to run a Half Marathon together. Kylie brought her trainers in that morning, putting them on her desk and loudly declaring she was going for a run after work.

Anna and Grace from probation were different. Kylie looked forward to the days they came to Phoenix to run the addiction group with her. Anna was strikingly beautiful - tall and willowy with curves in all the right places. She had enviable features that made women want to be her. Men were in awe of her beauty, knowing that she was completely unattainable. She was nice with it. Why couldn't she at least be a bitch? When Anna flashed a smile at you, it was as if you were the only person in the room. Grace was a nice girl, quiet, mousey, pleasant. She often deferred to Anna during conversations. Grace spotted Kylie's trainers on her desk, saying she was planning on running the Half Marathon herself and asked if Kylie would like to do it with her. Anna said she might join them for some training. That was all she needed - Anna sprinting along like a gazelle while she huffed and puffed, trying to keep up. She felt her skin prickling, the feeling of being watched as she allowed her thoughts to drift. When she looked up, Anna was watching her. Great, that's all I need thought, Kylie, Anna feeling sorry for me because I have no other friends to run with.

~

As Anna and Grace left Phoenix, there were a couple of dealers loitering outside as usual.

'Have you heard about the school mums?' Grace asked. Anna had, but she let Grace tell her about the school parents starting a petition - they were trying to get enough signatures to get the agency shut down – didn't want that kind of people loitering opposite the school.

'They won't get anywhere with it,' Anna shrugged, 'unless they deal drugs to the kids and someone dies, the authorities won't get involved. They are free to stand wherever they want. We all know something has to happen before anything changes.'

Luke

She smiled at him across the playground. Luke hated the thought of their flirtation being split by a playground; it made him sound like a pervert. He had seen her and her friends at one of the local clubs, Fuel, at the weekend. They spoke briefly in the smoking area, followed by a round of shots before the girls disappeared back into the sweaty mass of bodies on the dance floor. It wasn't somewhere he had expected to see her, and certainly not the sort of place he thought her well-to-do mother would know she had been. Mind you, the posh girls were always the worst for being party animals and usually filthy in bed as well, he thought, his mind drifting. Her mother dropped her off at school each morning, waving from her gleaming Range Rover. It annoyed Luke that it was always gleaming. Luke just hated those people that thought they were better than others because they had everything handed to them. He wondered what she would think if she knew her daughter was pissed and dancing the night away at Fuel last weekend. He gave Tilly a wink from his position outside Phoenix.

The police had been on at Luke since the mums were causing grief with that petition, but this spot was where he got some of his best customers, and he liked to see who was coming and going from the agency. If the police didn't catch him in the act, they couldn't touch him, and he wasn't stupid enough to have the gear on him. He knew how to play the game, and with a quick phone call, his customers could meet one of his boys around the corner to do the deal. He glanced back across the street to the school playground; Tilly was still watching him.

Luke planned to pay a visit to Fiona on the way home. He saw her leave the agency earlier, but two birds from probation left at the same time, and it wasn't worth the grief to try to catch her when they were around. She hadn't been using as much lately, and he was worried that she might have her head turned by the professionals sticking their noses in. He wanted to give a little incentive to make sure she wasn't tempted to try to cut down or give up. He would make the money back quickly as long as he kept her hooked. Addicts were all the same. Fiona was a good girl and always paid. She had always stuck to her morals and never gone on the game; he gave her credit for that, much as she would be a nice little earner for him if he could get her out with the rest of his girls. He took a cut from most of the girls in return for his protection – although most of the trouble was between the women themselves. All the feminist crap went out of the window when a good punter was up for grabs. Luke was respected in this city, with interests in lots of businesses. He liked it to be hassle-free, though didn't really care how he made his money as long as he got his cut out of it and no one made a mug out of him. He did occasionally experience a pang of remorse giving drugs to people like Fiona, but then reminded himself it is just business, and if he doesn't supply her, someone else will.

Fiona

Luke asked Fiona a while ago if she wanted to earn some extra cash doing cleaning work. It was easy money, cleaning for Luke's mum, Jackie. She was an amiable lady and seemed to appreciate Fiona's company as much as the help around the house. They enjoyed a cup of tea and Loose Women, debating alongside the show as if they were extra panellists. Jackie had old-fashioned values and told Fiona that when her husband had left them years ago, it was up to Luke to step up as the man of the house. As nice as she was, Fiona often wondered how Luke's life could have been different if his dad hadn't left or if his mum hadn't looked to him to provide for them. Luke's younger brother, James, was there sometimes, but she rarely saw him – if he wasn't at college, he was holed up in his room on his computer, the complete opposite to Luke. Fiona didn't clean his room; Jackie said to leave him to it. She was glad; something about James sent a shiver down her spine. Jackie often made sure Fiona had a good meal before she left and had become a sort of mother figure to her.

As she arrived back at her flat, the boy from across the hall was sitting on the stairs.

'Coming round to keep me company and take over my TV for a bit?' Dylan nodded. 'Your mum got a friend over?' He nodded again and got up, taking Fiona's bag from her. Her flat was so quiet with just her there, so she appreciated the company. She often invited him in when his mum was 'working'. He was a good kid. Sometimes if she had any extra money, she would get them chips from the takeaway. Fiona hadn't spoken to Dylan's Mum much. There was a steady stream of men coming and going, and it was obvious what line of work she was in. It must be hard for Dylan, but she understood his mum had to make money to keep the roof overhead in whatever way she could. Fiona knew too well that they all had choices to make in life.

Fiona started to feel a bit twitchy; she hadn't been using as much lately, but her addiction still reminded her when it was time for her next fix. She texted Luke saying she had been to his mum's this morning, and he replied saying he would drop the payment over later. Fiona was pleased, as this meant she could score at the same time. By the time Luke arrived, Dylan was home again.

Her

Here we go again, another welfare check on everyone's favourite addict. There were reports of thefts at several student houses recently, but nothing was proven because the teenagers had all been too drunk and out of it to give a halfway decent recollection of events. She knew who it was; she knew Fiona's MO, and enough was enough. *When would it end? No, she had had enough chances.*

She arrived at Fiona's flat before the cavalry got there. The door to the building was open, and she slipped in stealthily. As usual, Fiona's flat door wasn't locked, and with a quick glance around, she stepped inside. Fiona was out of it. It looked like she hadn't been out of the flat for days. The air was stale with lingering smoke, and her nose wrinkled at Fiona's bodily odours filling the small space. The silly girl could barely string a sentence together, lying on the sofa, her eyes rolling back in her head. She would have to act quickly.

Her pulse racing, she scooped up the items she needed from the coffee table – spoon, citric acid, lighter and syringe, deftly adding the citric acid and brown substance she had to the spoon. She flicked the lighter and held the flame underneath the dirty tea spoon until it bubbled. She drew the solution up into the syringe and paused, listening for sirens. Fiona's eyes were closed now, her body still and her chest rising and falling slowly.

Syringe loaded, she closed the gap between her and Fiona and turned her arm over in search of a vein. *Dammit. The veins there were no use. She ran her eyes over Fiona's body, the sound of a siren approaching. Quick. Think.* Her eyes fell upon Fiona's toe and the fresh track mark where she had recently injected. She plunged the needle into the same vein, wincing slightly and shuddering as she pushed the plunger in. Fiona's eyes flew open as the drugs raced towards her heart; her eyes filled with confusion when she saw her uninvited guest. There was no way Fiona's small body could survive the second dose that she had just been administered, and her body immediately started convulsing.

She stepped back, allowing herself a moment of regret she couldn't stick around and watch the exact moment the life left Fiona's body. As she stood there, the smell of Fiona's bowels hit her. She dropped the paraphernalia back where she found it and slipped back into the hallway just as she heard the loud steps and casual chatter as the rest of the professionals arrived. She posed herself so it looked as though she had arrived moments before and had not yet entered the flat.

'Here we go again,' she said with a wry smile to the others, 'this girl has more lives than a cat. Thank goodness she has people looking out for her. Good day so far?'

The Professionals

'I know we aren't supposed to get attached, but she was one of my favourites,' Emma sobbed, 'we all knew it could happen any day, but I suppose I just hoped it wouldn't.' Tom was at the Social Services office with Emma. Sensing an opportunity, he put his hand on her knee, passing her a tissue.

'Shall we get out of here?'

Emma nodded tearfully and sent a message to Beth saying she was leaving early.

Fiona had been found deceased, still warm, but her heart had stopped beating when they entered the property. Even though she had overdosed before, they usually got there in time. Once the toxicology results were back, there would be an Adult Safeguarding Review. This would be Emma's first, and her stomach fluttered at the thought of the investigation. Her notes were up to date, and this wasn't something she could have foreseen, even though it wasn't entirely unexpected. This didn't stop the anxiety from building in the pit of her stomach. She smiled at Tom as they left the building, her stomach fluttering for a different reason.

~

Kylie busied herself printing flyers warning about the dangers of overdose with a list of top tips to inspire the clients to stay alive – know your tolerance, buy from a 'reputable dealer', don't share needles, all the usual gumph, etc. She grabbed a staple gun and headed out of the office to the public areas to decorate the group rooms, waiting areas, and hallways with the flyers. She knew this was one hazard of the job, but it didn't make it any easier. This was the first time she had lost a client, and she had a meeting with her manager later to go over her notes. She felt sick. Even though she knew she had done all she could, she couldn't help thinking there must have been something else she could have done.

'Is it true, Kylie?' Word was spreading, and she had been told she couldn't confirm anything yet. She dropped her eyes to the floor and mumbled something about not being able to give out information before scurrying away. As she passed through the waiting area to return to the office, the receptionist handed her a bulky envelope and asked if she could take it up to the main office. It was postmarked from the company sponsoring the Half Marathon event - clearly, she wouldn't be getting any invite to run with her colleagues. She was going for a run with Grace and Anna next week. Stuff those bitches.

Marie

Marie thought that with Carl gone, life would be easier, but it was so quiet when the kids were asleep, and her bed felt cold and empty. Carl's company, even when hostile, was still company. She berated herself for missing him, frowning and taking a deep breath as her heart strings pulled. The bruises had healed, and she no longer wore a bandage on her hand, the shiny scar looking less angry as each day passed.

Marie had formally identified Carl's body and collected his personal items, putting them in the understairs cupboard, out of sight until now. She took a deep breath and opened the sealed plastic packet. There wasn't much in there - wallet, wedding ring, watch, phone, cigarettes and a lighter. She felt the tears threatening to start as she clutched his wedding ring in her palm. She plugged his phone into her charger, waiting for it to power up, then seeing the notifications appear. It surprised her it didn't have a password, but then it never left his side, and she wouldn't have dared to look at it before. Marie felt as though he might walk in at any moment and catch her snooping. She tentatively cleared the missed calls and saw several apps she didn't recognise at first - Bumble, Hinge, Tinder. She felt like she couldn't catch her breath, closing her eyes. All those times he had come home in the middle of the night, the scent of perfume on his body, she knew in her heart what he had been up to, but she wanted to believe his lies. It was easier.

Marie opened her eyes. She didn't open the unread text messages or other notifications. Fuck you, Carl, she thought as she threw his phone across the room. It cracked as it hit the fireplace, and she saw the shattered screen as it lay on the floor. He wasn't the perfect husband; he looked at other women in front of her, often pointing out her flaws in comparison, but this confirmation snapped something inside her. Feeling a weight lifted, she shouted up to the girls that they would have McDonald's for dinner later as a treat.

Beth, the Social Worker, was due soon. Marie put the kettle on and laid chocolate digestives out on a plate. She helped herself to a biscuit safe knowing that Carl wouldn't catch her and suggest an apple instead. Marie hoped Carl's death would mean Social Services would stop coming, but Beth said she was keeping her file open for a short period as a supportive measure.

The girls seemed to cope surprisingly well without Carl in their lives and had accepted that Daddy had gone to live in the sky with their rabbit, Thumper. Marie told them whilst they couldn't see Daddy, he would always look down on them and watch out for them. Alice said she thought that would be nice because she could still show him her drawings. Her heart broke when Alice asked if he would still make mummy cry all the time now he is in heaven.

~

'How are you coping? Is there anything I can do? It can't be easy doing everything on your own.' Carl's friend, John, had dropped by with some work boots Carl had left in his car.

56

'Here,' he held out the boots, without waiting for an answer, 'I didn't want to throw them out; it's not my place.'

'We are getting there, thank you,' Marie said as she took the boots and went to shut the door.

'Wait. Do you need a hand with anything while I am here? Might as well make myself useful.' Marie hesitated. John put his hand on the door, and she stepped back, gesturing for him to step past her into the hallway.

John put the bins out, fixed the wobbly hall table and changed the light bulb on the landing. He said to call if she ever needed anything, and she wondered if it might be nice to invite him along for McDonald's with the girls to say thank you. She'd been asking Carl to change that bulb for weeks.

Luke

Tilly broke away from her usual position with her friends and strode across the playground. With a quick glance around, she slipped out the school gates and in his direction. What was it about girls in school uniform? His eyes were always drawn to her, intrigued and fascinated, attracted to her confidence.

'Give me your phone,' she said. He looked at her. 'Phone,' she demanded, holding out her hand. She handed it back immediately for him to enter his password. 'Friday night,' she said, 'text me, and I'll tell you where to pick me up.' She turned and walked back in the direction of the school gates. She didn't look back. He kept his eyes focused on her until she disappeared from view.

Friday came around quickly, and Luke booked a table at the Speckled Pig. He was picking Tilly up from her friend's house, where she had told her mum she would spend the night. He pulled up in a taxi and saw her face appear at the upstairs window. She looked incredible. Luke was not used to women making an effort. Tilly was the opposite of the women he was used to dealing with day to day. Her long hair hung loose, and he breathed in the coconut scent as she flicked it over her shoulder as she got in the back seat of the taxi alongside him. She wore a sparkling sequined mini dress and flashed him that smile of hers, the one that made his heart beat faster and his trousers tighter.

Luke ordered a bottle of champagne, and they sat in the bar, waiting for their table to be ready. He couldn't tear his eyes from Tilly, soaking in every detail, watching her drink the champagne, her cheeks slightly pink.

'Let's dance,' she said suddenly, grabbing his hand and pulling him to the small dance floor in the bar area. The dining tables were busy, but there was no one else on the dance floor. She danced around him; her energy made the air crackle. She didn't take her eyes from his. When the waitress interrupted, saying their table was ready, Tilly dismissed her with a wave, saying they were no longer hungry. She grabbed his hand and led him outside, suggesting they go dancing instead. Luke couldn't decide if she had taken something or if this was Tilly. Either way, he wanted to know more. They went to another bar; they drank more champagne, and she swayed in time with the music. Sometimes Luke would watch from the edge of the dance floor. It felt like there was no one else in the room, and she was putting on a private show for him.

It was midnight, and Tilly danced her way towards him. Her eyes shone, and her dress sparkled in the moonlight. She leaned in close, and he breathed in her musky scent, his hair standing on end as she whispered in his ear, 'Good Night, Luke', before giving him a peck on the cheek and disappearing into the crowd.

Luke looked around the club and couldn't see her. He pushed through the crowded dance floor of the club and emerged into the cool air, seeing a flash of sequins in the back of a taxi disappearing into the night. He let out the breath he was holding.

~

Midnight was still early in his world, and while he was out, Luke thought he may as well check on business. A nice evening like this, he should make a good wedge from the working girls. He passed by Fiona's block of flats on the way to his destination, thinking how lucky he was that the police hadn't been able to connect him to the drugs following her overdose. She was a good steady customer, not a bad sort, but in his experience, once the drugs got hold of you, there was rarely a way back. Docker Street was busy, the girls milling around, allowing the punters to crawl along until they saw something they wanted. Police turned a blind eye as long as there was no trouble. Things generally ran smoothly, and his boys stopped by regularly. They had a flat nearby, where they did business, and the girls would drop their takings off. They could also score whatever they needed to keep them high enough to get the job done. Even if they started this work thinking they were in control and without a habit, Luke had been in the game long enough to know their soul would soon break, and they would inevitably turn to drugs. No matter how much Luke and his boys monitored things, they couldn't see everything, and they couldn't always get there in time. It would start with the odd pill or sniff here and there to get through the act itself, then maybe a pick me up later in the night and something after work to chill out and get to sleep. Eventually, the powders would stop giving the desired hit, and they would start asking for something stronger. Once they were pinning up, that was it. One of the hardest parts of the job was balancing how much to let them use. You had to keep them at the right level of addiction. You didn't want them looking too strung out. Even the most desperate punters had a limit.

Her

She got away with it. Twice. She monitored the news for any story hinting at suspected foul play in Carl or Fiona's deaths, and there was nothing. She scrolled through social media, reading the tributes posted by their friends. *Why was it that as soon as someone died, no one had a bad word to say about them? No-one said they were glad there was one less wife-beater ruining the lives of those around him. No-one said how good it was that his wife was now free, and his children would no longer have to grow up in that toxic environment. They should thank her for her service to the community, not post tributes to a wonderful husband and father.* The newspaper picked up the story with the tragic accident angle giving it the headline 'Family man taken too soon'. As for Fiona, the tributes declared an angel had gained her wings, that she was too good for this world. *No! The world was better than her. She was given chance after chance to sort herself out, and she continued to be a fuckup, wasting the time and energy of everyone in her orbit. Her parents must have been so ashamed of her; at least now they could say she was dead.*

It had been surprisingly easy. She felt invincible. It was so hard to act normally – she wanted to share this high with someone. Wanted to share that she had got rid of a couple of wasters and bask in the thanks and admiration that she deserved.

She often paused to think about how her life would be different if she had someone to share it with. Aside from a few distant cousins, she was on her own. She supposed there would be people on her father's side, but she had never known her father. Her mother said it was a fling and he wasn't ready to be a dad, so she ended the relationship and moved away, never telling him. When her mother died, she had found letters amongst her mother's belongings telling him he had a daughter. There was no name or address to give her a clue as to how to find him. Her mother always said, one day, she would take her to him. She never did, and her father's identity died along with her mother. *If her mother hadn't died as she had, would she still feel the urge to purge society?*

Alas, she must go to work and show compassion, do nothing to draw attention to how good she feels inside. Business as usual.

The Professionals

Kylie and Grace were running the group today, and they had been tasked with formally letting the group know that Fiona had passed away. Most of them already knew, news spread quickly with social media. They talked about loss in the session.

Grace was working her way around the room, checking in, asking how everyone's week had been. Frank said his week was okay, and he was proud of the changes he made to his drinking. Bullshit, thought Kylie. The sour aroma of stale alcohol clung to him, giving away his secrets.

A couple of the girls sobbed through check-in, declaring how sad it was without Fiona. Frank spoke about how loss made him think of his old life and everything he had before he started drinking. They all spoke about what they could do instead of drink or drugs to cope with life.

~

Work finished for the day, Kylie and Grace got changed and headed out for a run. They had quickly fallen into a routine of running once a week after group. Even if they weren't both running the group that day, they would meet in the car park behind the building. Kylie learned that Grace was the oldest child of five. She still lived with her parents, who were older, and did a lot for them while her siblings were off travelling or having families. It seemed to Grace that Kylie was the long-suffering sort who would always be taken advantage of.

As they ran, Kylie and Grace settled into a steady pace and a companionable silence. They both noticed Frank in the beer garden of Wetherspoons as they ran by. Neither one said anything. They didn't need to. They ran along The Barbican and past the forgotten police tape where the body had been found last week.

'He was on Anna's caseload,' Grace said as they passed the tape flapping in the wind.

'Oh no, is she okay?' asked Kylie, concerned.

'Unflappable as always,' Grace puffed as they rounded the corner, starting the incline up the hill from The Barbican alongside the water towards Plymouth Hoe.

~

Tom walked into the bedroom with a towel around his hips as Emma pulled her jacket on. She ran her fingers through her hair, facing the mirror to apply a fresh coat of lipstick. He came up behind her wrapping his arms around her waist and nuzzling her neck. She felt him getting excited again and twisted away.

'I have to go; I'm going with Beth to do a couple of visits on the way home. Her team are short-staffed, and they need two people for some cases, so I said I'd go.' She glanced back at the rumpled sheets, the pillow hanging off the edge of the bed, and grinned, thinking of their afternoon screwing. She resisted the urge to tidy the bed. It felt exciting, sneaking off in the middle of the day to spend a couple of satisfying hours getting to know each other. She wished they could have spent the night together after their first time. She pushed thoughts of his wife aside, ignoring the queasiness in her stomach. Running her eyes over Tom's nearly naked body one last time, her cheeks flushed as she tore herself away.

Tom thought he might keep the room key and not check out yet. He may as well get his money's worth and would if the wife fancied a bunk up later if they could get a babysitter. As Emma made her way down in the lift, Tom rang Reception to ask if someone could nip up and make up the room before he got back later. He would pick up a bottle of fizz and some flowers from the Spar shop - no chance was he paying hotel prices. He would get prosecco and put it in the hotel ice bucket to look like he had splashed out on champagne. His wife would never check. He texted Katie to say he was on the way back to the station and rang his wife.

~

Emma met Beth at the property and asked for a quick update on who they were seeing.

'Long-term marriage to an abusive husband, always refused to press charges or make a statement, twin girls. You know the body that was found on The Barbican? That was him. The visit is just a check-in to see how things are going. Hopefully, I can close the case soon now that the husband has gone.'

Their conversation was brought to a halt as their knock at the door was answered. Beth looked at the man who answered the door. He smiled, his eyes twinkling as if he had just been laughing at something, and he held his hand out, introducing himself as John. He ushered them into the living room, offering drinks. Beth sighed. Marie appeared in the living room a couple of minutes later with cups of tea and sat on the sofa. Her cheeks were rosy; she had a hint of makeup on and wore a pretty blouse and skirt. Beth had never seen Marie wearing makeup before. She made eye contact with Marie and raised one eyebrow wordlessly.

'Carl's friend, John,' she said by explanation, 'he has been great since it happened, helping around the house and with the kids. I don't know how we would have managed without him.'

'He seems to have made himself at home,' observed Beth. They discussed Marie's Care Plan, with Beth noting no further police call-outs and no evidence to suggest risk to the children's welfare. The school had no concerns, and the children seemed to cope relatively well, given the loss of their dad. Children in homes with domestic abuse always proved to be resilient.

They raised the subject of John again, and Marie assured Beth she was not looking for a relationship. 'He is just a friend'.

'I will send you one more appointment, just to make sure things are okay, but the case was opened due to the nature of your relationship with Carl, so I see no reason we can't close it soon, providing nothing else crops up,' Beth said, looking pointedly at John as he came in to offer everyone another drink. Her eyes flicked to John's hand as he squeezed Marie's shoulder on the way past.

'What do you reckon?' Beth asked Emma when they were out of earshot of the house.

'He was very comfortable there. If they're not already shagging, they soon will be.'

'Talking of shagging…. How was lunch with Tom?' Before Emma could answer, Beth added, 'oh, and before you try to deny anything, you were off the grid this afternoon, and you are missing an earring, so don't even try to leave out any details. I am old and married and need to live vicariously through you.'

Emma put her hand to her ear lobe, frowning. 'Shit.' She grabbed her phone, googling the number for the hotel. They were a 21st birthday present from her mum. The hotel Receptionist said they would have to call Tom as it was his name on the booking but assured her they would look and let him know.

Her

Running at night gave her freedom and anonymity that she loved. She ran taking everything in, her senses heightened, but invisible to others as she ran in the darkness. She glanced in the mirror as she left the house, her blonde hair pulled back into a functional ponytail emphasising her features. The shadows across her face highlighted the cheekbones she got from her mother.

The first time she ran was the night her mother died. She left the house and ran. She intended to step outside and think, but as soon as her feet hit the pavement, she broke into a run. It felt like she ran for hours, tears streaming down her face. When she stopped, gasping for air, pain ripping through her insides, she saw the stark reality of the world she lived in. Her breathlessness subsided as she took deep breaths, ignoring looks from passers-by at the sweaty, tearful teenager. She was alone. Not one person stopped to ask if she was okay. Her eyes followed the path of the people who crossed the road or looked down to avoid her eye contact – anything to ensure they didn't have to get involved. There was a moment – a moment where she realised, she could be alone, or she could be *alone,* and she had a choice. Straightening up, pulling her shoulders back and re-tying her hair, she walked home.

Since that day, running was an escape or a space to think – whatever she wanted it to be. She broke into a run as soon as she hit the pavement outside the house and ran toward town. It was early evening, and people had yet to draw the curtains allowing her to glimpse into their private worlds, running past house after house. The roads were quiet; most people were home from work, any businesses long closed for the night. She ran past the flats where Fiona lives. Lived, she corrected her thoughts with a smirk. There was a boy kicking a ball at a fence by the side of the building. She was light on her feet, and her rubber soles allowed her to remain silent and invisible. She passed a derelict car park, soon to be demolished. The commercial building attached was deserted, with closing down sale signs still visible in the windows. The car park had become a place for the homeless to congregate. She saw them in the shadows, huddled together, the occasional orange glow of a cigarette as someone took a drag. The Rough Sleeper Teams would visit the car park at dawn, providing food and water and checking in on the regulars. The door to homelessness was revolving, and some people just didn't want to be helped. She had seen so many of these pathetic addicts offered accommodation only to mess it up. One of the most frustrating scenarios was when the women wouldn't take accommodation unless their shithead abusive boyfriends could come with them. So many chose to stay homeless *with* their boyfriend over a safe place to stay without him.

The strange camaraderie and companionship that formed among the addicts and the homeless was fascinating. It gave their community a familial sense of loyalty – unless someone ran out of crack, then all bets were off.

She found herself on the street Marie lived on. Feeling curious, she ran towards the house and hovered in the shadows of a tree opposite, catching a glimpse in the

69

illuminated window. She felt justified and altruistic in despatching of Carl as she observed the smiling face of Marie laughing at something. The girls chatted and ate pizza from takeaway boxes. If it wasn't for her, Marie would still be the old Marie, pale and withdrawn. She would still be living in fear, and those children would have Carl as a father. She turned and ran, retracing her steps, satisfied her work there was done. If she had stayed a few seconds longer, she would have seen John sitting down to eat with them.

Frank

Since his release from prison, Frank couldn't avoid seeing the faces of people as they passed him in the street – some would cross the road, avoiding eye contact, and others glared at him with no attempt to conceal their contempt. In prison, the other prisoners didn't bother him too much - his crime was minor compared to many others. That didn't stop the officers from referring to him as The Child Killer. This was his life now; he would forever be a child killer. Future employers, girlfriends and friends would only have to Google him to see the full details of what happened, though most people around here knew the story already. He was no longer just Frank; he was Frank who had to tick a box, Frank with a criminal record. He sometimes wished he was back in prison. At least then, they were all stuck in limbo together. Not being able to move forward was easier than constant rejection.

Frank didn't fit in with the criminals, but he no longer fit in with his old friends. They didn't know what to say to him. They would make vague and awkward references to his time away as if he lived overseas rather than acknowledge that he was in prison for killing two school girls. Prison was the elephant in the room, and the unspoken agreement was not to mention it.

Since release, he felt like every day he was on a miserable autopilot, a crappy version of the 90s film, the Truman Show, where Jim Carey was stuck living the same day over and over. Every day, Frank visited the library scouring the job adverts online, avoiding his mum with her endless well-meaning cups of tea and fussing. He stayed at the library as long as he could handle the silence, before going to the pub in the afternoon and home for tea. On the days he had to see probation or go to his addiction group at Phoenix, he tried to wait until later before he had a drink.

Today, Frank had an appointment at probation. He hated going there. He hated how the way the professionals looked at him in the waiting room with a mixture of disgust and pity. In his old life, he was a professional. He was one of them, and now he was nothing. A criminal. A killer. Frank shared the waiting room with a young lad who reeked of cannabis. The others always eyed him with suspicion, as he didn't fit in with their type. Fiona once told him that the normal-looking people at probation were usually nonces, the normal-looking people and old men. Since all the business with Jimmy Savile, there were a lot of older men coming in the waiting room as people were speaking up about things that happened years ago. Fiona seemed to genuinely care that people were coming forward and reporting their experiences – she had had a good heart. He remembered how she laughed when she said the downside was that prison and probation offices looked like nursing homes. After she told him this, he always wanted to say to the others that he wasn't a paedophile just in case that was what they thought, but then that would make it sound like he was.

Anna was right on time for Frank's appointment and led him to one of the little interview rooms, taking a seat across from him, a personal alarm sitting on the desk in front of her. He liked Anna and found her to be firm but fair compared to probation officers he had worked with in prison. Anna asked if he was drinking again. Frank hesitated before saying he had the odd drink with a meal, but it was under control. She asked how he was finding the course at Phoenix so far and how life was going in general. He broke down and said he just wanted to move on with his life and stop feeling like life was just a tick in a box.

'Are you feeling like you want to end your life?' Anna asked. She followed up with the required series of questions necessary for her to assess if there was any imminent risk of suicide. Anna was going to make an appointment for him to see a specialist careers advisor and put a referral in for him to have some one-to-one counselling, but the wait list was long, she said. In the meantime, he should keep doing what he was doing and ring the helpline number she gave him if he felt suicidal.

To his credit, Frank avoided the pub on the way home. Unfortunately, he also had to pass a corner shop, where he filled his bag with eight cans of beer and a bottle of whiskey. He went straight to his bedroom and drank until he went to bed with just the silence for company.

Marie

John was becoming a regular visitor to Marie and the girls. Nothing ever happened between them, and Marie was grateful for this. She thought of Carl and pushed aside the thoughts that she might like it to happen. She had never been on her own, having been with Carl since they were at school. She didn't like it, but despite this, was apprehensive at the thought of anything new. John often popped in on the way home from work with colouring books for the girls or a takeaway for them all. He did jobs around the house and mowed the lawn when it needed it. She didn't know what she would do without him. John took them all to a family theme park with a zoo at the weekend. He paid for their tickets - two adults and two children – a Family Ticket. She felt a pang of guilt at that. Later, he gave her a voucher for a salon in town and said it wasn't just the kids who deserved a treat. John was so generous and thoughtful with his money. Her stomach lurched with butterflies when she got a message from him or saw his familiar face approaching. John felt too good to be true.

When she thought about it, Carl never spoke about him much other than to say that John gave him a lift to work some days, so she didn't actually know anything about him. She didn't like to ask too much as John spoke about Carl as if they were best friends, so it felt rude to ask. That was how it was with Carl anyway; he had his life and his friends, and didn't share his world with her. Marie pushed thoughts of Carl out of her mind, grateful for the attention from John. After all, not many men would be interested in spending their weekends with a single mum with two young girls, not without getting something in return, anyway.

When John had gone home and the girls were in bed, Marie often lay awake, her brain refusing to switch off, thinking about Carl. She remembered when they were young and happy and wracked her mind for signs that it was going wrong. Was there anything she could have done for this to have ended differently? He was her husband, and her stomach twisted when she thought about her betrayal with the feelings lingering for John. Sometimes, she would get out of bed to check the door was locked, in case Carl was still alive and it was all a big horrible understanding, in case John was a test.

The Professionals

Katie popped into Social Services to check on some joint cases. She preferred to go in person for a cup of tea and a natter when she had the time.

'Case closed,' Beth said when Katie asked for an update on Marie. 'There's no reason to suspect any imminent risk of harm to the children, although there is a new bloke hanging around. We had a chat about the impact of the children seeing a new relationship so soon, and she's aware she needs to put their needs first. Ran a check on him, and nothing came back. Who's next on the list?'

Katie ran through a few other cases they were both working with. They spoke about Dylan, the young boy often seen out and about on his own, who lived in the block of flats at the bottom of town. Beth said he had been placed with his grandparents many times but kept running back to his mum's. Dylan's mum was a known sex worker, and the lad was often seen outside the building when she was working. The trouble with the slightly older children was that they voted with their feet, and short of locking him in his grandparent's house, they couldn't make him stay there. All they could do was monitor him. Katie said she'd speak to some of the other patrols to raise awareness just so they could try to keep an eye out for him when in the area. Dylan's mum was currently drug-free and on a Methadone Script. She was engaging with Sally at Revive, which was something, although she was very clear that she was only going as she was told she had to or they would take away her Methadone. Beth didn't care why she went; just getting her in the door would give Sally a good chance of getting some meaningful work completed. Dylan's mum was clearly a resourceful woman, and with the right motivation and support, perhaps there was another way of life for her.

Katie attended a 999 call the day before and found a young woman in her bathtub, many cuts visible on her arms through the red water. The call came from the woman's daughter, who was dropped home by another parent when her mum didn't turn up for school pick up. The daughter could not get in the bathroom but could hear the tap running and ended up calling the police. Luckily, Katie's colleague was able to keep the girl talking in the living room while Katie gained access and took in the gruesome scene. Katie finished her cup of tea with Beth and went in search of an update from the Social Worker who attended the suicide and took the child to an emergency foster care placement.

She got a text from Tom saying he was on shift in half an hour, asking if he should meet her at the station or out and about. She tapped a quick reply saying she was at Social Services and had the car and if he could get another patrol to drop him there, it would save her going back to collect him.

Katie was relieved to find out that the girl from yesterday had been moved from the emergency foster placement to a temporary kinship carer but that this was not a long-term solution. She was grateful that she could work alongside many other agencies, and they had all formed an alliance as colleagues. It made the harder parts easier to process, as she could find out what happened next. It was not always a happy ending, but sometimes not knowing was the worst bit. Of course, many times in this job, she would never know. There would be familiar faces that they saw regularly until that one day, they just disappeared. They would often never know if they had moved away and sorted themselves out, or died. There would never be an answer or an ending to the story that started for her with the 999 call. She hoped she would get to follow up on the outcome of this poor kid.

~

Tom and Emma left Emma's house where they had met for 'lunch', AKA a quickie. Her house was central, and it was convenient when her son was at school. She kept asking to see his place, but his wife was there. Tom said they were in separate rooms whilst they sorted out the separation. Luckily, she accepted this for now.

Emma followed Tom's car to the station and then drove him to meet Katie. Katie was just coming out of the building with her phone in her hand when he and Emma parked up. Katie looked at him with one eyebrow raised as he sauntered over to her but said nothing.

Dylan's mum

'Be a good boy and go to the shop and get some milk,' Dylan's mum said as she handed him a £5 note. He knew the score and pushed the money into his pocket as he left the flat. On the way out, he passed a smartly dressed man he had seen before who winked at him. He heard his mum's laughter echoing through the hall as she greeted the man. Dylan sat on the steps outside. He didn't bother to go to the shop; there was fresh milk in the fridge. He missed Fiona. No-one else in the building spoke to him. They stepped around him wordlessly on the way in and out. The only acknowledgement that he was there was the occasional glance of pity. People scurried past as if his crappy life was catching; not that many of theirs were much better. People didn't want to get involved. He sat watching the rest of the world go by - the occasional car, a man with a dog, the reflection of blue flashing lights somewhere in the distance. He saw a woman in black running; some of her blonde hair had escaped her hairband and was dancing behind her in the moonlight. His eyes flickered in recognition of her profile as she ran through the spotlight of the streetlight, but he couldn't quite place her.

Dylan looked at his watch as the man in the suit left the building.

He winked at Dylan again and said, 'quite the woman, your mum,' before getting into his BMW and driving off. Dylan squeezed his eyes and his fists tightly closed, his grubby fingernails digging into his palms. He breathed out and made his way back up to the flat, the smell of fresh smoke mixed with sweat and something else greeted him. His mum wore a short dressing gown with the cord tied securely at her waist. He avoided eye contact and put the oven on, tipping half a bag of chicken nuggets onto an oven tray and squeezing a dollop of mayonnaise on his plate before eyeing up the dishes that needed doing.

Dylan knew what his mum was. When he was younger, he didn't understand why the men were coming and going. His mum told him to stay in his room, and he used to hide under the duvet until she came and told him to come out. He heard grunting and shrieks and felt frightened. Now he always left the flat. As he got older, the other kids at school would say things about his mum. At first, he didn't understand. He had never had a dad and didn't know that it wasn't usual for there to be so many men in and out of his mum's bedroom. He knew something wasn't right but still thought it was the same for everyone until the other kids spoke about their mums and dads. No matter what they said about her, she was still his mum, and he loved her. She did her best for them. He tried to help around the house so she had less to worry about. For now, she was off the drugs, and mostly, she was happier. Sometimes she took him to the park, or they got fish and chips. Whenever the man in the green car with the silver jaguar on the bonnet came to visit, she gave him a £10 note to spend on whatever he wanted. Dylan kept them carefully hidden away for the next time she went back on the drugs, so he could top up the electric and get food for them.

Her

She ran her fingers gently through her freshly curled hair before rubbing conditioning serum on the ends. Her dress hugged her body in all the right places, and her curves were accentuated by a flat stomach and toned legs. She pulled a leather jacket on and grabbed her handbag, sliding her feet into her favourite heels to complete the outfit. One last look in the mirror to check her makeup, not that it was ever anything but flawless, and she headed to the waiting taxi. She had given in to cajoling from her friends and colleagues and was off on a Tinder date. The app could be fun to swipe away on, but it was also rather depressing. Most of the cretins on there seemed to think they were god's gift when they clearly left much to be desired. She saw profiles of men she knew were in relationships and people she knew to be convicted abusers, addicts or just general assholes. When she widened her search radius, she even saw one profile for someone she knew was a serving prisoner at HMP Dartmoor; she sent a screenshot of his profile to her friend who worked there in security.

She wasn't sure what to expect from tonight, but the guy seemed normal, and it got her out of the house. As soon as the taxi dropped her at the bar, she spotted him standing outside, looking slightly awkward. She paid her driver and stepped towards her date in greeting. He held open the bar door and gestured for her to step inside. She appreciated chivalry. The place wasn't busy, and they were shown to a table outside with views over Plymouth Sound. The bar was in the Prestigious Royal William Yard, which had views of the River Tamar and Plymouth Sound. She considered living in one of the beautiful old military buildings on the edge of the area but decided on somewhere a little less lively. The sky was turning beautiful shades of reds, pinks and oranges, all reflecting off the water. The daytime visitors to the area and its abundance of restaurants and cafes were heading off, and the evening crowd were being drawn in for drinking and dancing. Their spot on the terrace was perfect for people-watching. She eyed the groups of girls out for civilised drinks before the inevitable dancing and silliness began, the couples out for date nights – older couples retired and enjoying a new lease of life, couples freshly in lust, who were seeing where the night would take them, and the mums and dads out for a night out away from the kids. You could spot the new parents a mile off, realising that beyond the children, they didn't have much to say to each other whilst anxiously checking their phones every five minutes, hoping the babysitter couldn't cope without them.

She had never wanted children. Family life was over-rated. As she scanned the area, she spotted Tom crossing the cobbled street. Her eyes followed the direction he was looking, but she couldn't quite see who he was meeting. Her date pulled her attention back to the table, asking what she thought of the wine. He had selected a Cabernet Sauvignon, and she swirled the wine in the glass, breathing in the fruity aroma before enjoying a sip of the full-bodied Bordeaux. She chided herself for having let her mind drift and brought her focus back to the date. She knew he was a divorced father to two teenage girls and owned his own accountancy firm from the app. He showed her pictures of his daughters, and she recognised the uniform of the school across the road from Phoenix. He asked about her work now, and she skilfully turned the conversation back to his daughters, asking if either of them had shown an interest in following in his footsteps to work in his firm. Parents were always the same, so easy to distract from questions she didn't want to answer by asking about their kids.

The date was actually okay, and she enjoyed herself. She knew he would call her for a second date. They always did. She enjoyed making bets with herself on how long they could wait before calling her. This one seemed keen but not in a needy way. She smiled and waved as she got in the taxi, predicting that he would be in touch this evening.

At home, she stepped out of her heels, hung her jacket on the hook behind the door and left her earrings in a bowl on the hall table. She wandered into the kitchen, mindlessly filling the cat bowl with food while the kettle bubbled. The herbs by the window were dry, and she watered them, noticing the white flowers on her Lily of the Valley wilting, ready to be replaced with the plush red berries. The plant was supposed to signify happiness, purity, and humility. It was in Kate Middleton's bouquet at the royal wedding some years ago. Despite being a popular flower, it was surprisingly toxic, and she took care to wash her hands after pruning. She rubbed some of the lemon thyme between her fingertips, enjoying the fresh scent. Her mother garnered so much joy from plants – taking care of them was one of the threads holding the memories of time spent together, smelling flowers and laughing in the garden. She was so full of sunshine when she wasn't ill.

Her phone pinged on the worktop, and she saw he had already texted her, asking if she was home safely. She tapped a quick reply saying yes and thanking him for the evening before dropping her phone in her bag and heading for bed with a cup of chamomile tea. She knew all the dating handbooks would say she should not have replied so quickly, but she really couldn't be doing with all the games dating involved these days. Humans were such interesting creatures with the games they play. It would probably go a long way to explaining why people managed to get away with such poor, unaccountable behaviour.

The
Professionals

Tom's wife suggested they go out for a meal for their anniversary. Since the baby, she had made little effort and seemed annoyed if Tom even thought about sex, let alone went near her. She turned down his attempt to get things back on track in the hotel and said it was too short notice. He hoped tonight was the start of things turning around, as he couldn't put up with this forever. Emma was pushing him for commitment, and he was feeling smothered. She thought he was separated, and he wasn't sure it would go down well to tell her the truth now. He had been here before. He just wanted a bit of fun, and women always wanted more. The last one had turned into a total nut job. Luckily, she was off work on long-term sick, so he didn't have to see her.

Tom and his wife had a lovely meal at Royal William Yard. She even had a few drinks. He could almost remember what things used to be like before episiotomies and nappies changed his world. Things were going well until the journey home. She suddenly became quiet, and the atmosphere was strained.

'Everything okay?' He asked, concerned that his chances of getting his leg over might be diminishing.

'I'm just tired, not used to drinking and missing the baby,' she said, her head turned to look out of the window as he drove.

When they got home, she left him to pay the babysitter and went straight to bed. Confused by the sudden shift but not ready to face her cold shoulder, Tom poured himself a generous measure of whiskey. When he eventually went to bed, the room was in darkness. With a sigh, he quietly left his clothes in a heap and got into bed. The next morning, she didn't say a word, and Tom left without breakfast.

~

It was Tom and Grace facilitating the group, and the topic was relationships. Neither of them felt best placed to offer much insight to this one. Tom's texts to his wife had gone unanswered throughout the day, the blue ticks on WhatsApp showing they had been read. Grace was eternally single. She went on the odd date, but they never seemed to go anywhere. The group members were asked to consider the relationships they had in their life. Frank spoke about his mum - 'All I do is let her down.' He spoke of his loneliness and desire for human touch. They asked the other group members about their relationships. Matt, the lad who had been in a pub fight, lived at home with his mum and dad, no partner. He spoke about his dad's military career and growing up in a home rigid with rules and regime for months on end, followed by a sigh of relief when his dad went away, and they could all relax. His dad had never laid a hand on them, he said, but Matt said he always felt it was a possibility, an unspoken threat. A few others in the group spoke out, and it ended up being an insightful group session. When they came out of the group, Tom had a couple of missed calls on his mobile from Katie and a text asking him to call her.

'I've had your wife on the phone, Tom, and I've just lied for you. Don't you ever put me in that position again,' Katie seethed down the phone.

Tom's heartbeat quickened, 'What happened?'

'She found an earring in your car, in a Premier Inn envelope. You idiot.' Tom's heart sank to his stomach. He picked up the earring Emma left at the hotel and forgot to give it to her. His wife must have seen it when she was looking for mints in the glove box on the way home last night.

'I told her it was mine, and I was too embarrassed to pick it up after a one-night stand. She didn't sound convinced, but if you stick to the story, you might win her around.'

Tom breathed a sigh of relief. 'I owe you one.'

'You owe me more than one.'

He pulled out his phone and texted his wife again, confident now he knew what had happened, saying he would pick up a takeaway and a bottle of wine on the way home. He would get some flowers as well.

When Tom got home, his wife was still standoffish, but she was definitely coming around. He decided not to mention the earring and busied himself in the kitchen, getting out plates and wine glasses while she checked on the baby. He lit some of the nice scented candles she seemed obsessed with buying and poured the wine as she came back into the kitchen/ diner.

'You'd better not be at it again. I told you, after last time, we will leave. We deserve better than this.'

'You're imagining things. You know my girls are my world. Why would I want anyone else?'

She pursed her lips, staring at him, then sighed and took a sip of wine he offered. She always came round eventually. Tom and his wife were childhood sweethearts. He had been in the cool group at school, the preppy boys who played a lot of sports and all the girls fancied. She was quiet, studious, her beauty innocuous and unassuming. They were devoted in high school but went to different universities. When they came home in holidays, it became clear they were living very different university experiences. She overlooked his party lifestyle, and he vowed to be faithful once they finished uni. When he proposed, he said to his friend she would be faithful once they were married. By the time they were married, she was used to looking the other way.

Luke

Luke was at the school gates waiting for Tilly to finish. He wanted to take her to an actual restaurant and spend time with her rather than just drinking. He had it bad. He had never wanted to actually talk to a woman before. Sure, he didn't mind a bit of talk before taking them to bed, but the motivation was always sex. He rarely slept with the same woman twice. Tilly was different; she had class, unlike the women he was used to. She was the kind of girl that got under your skin, making you want her to stick around and have pillow talk. She was the first-person Luke had even thought about introducing to his mum.

When Luke's dad walked out on them, he had to step up and be the man of the house. His mum sobbed for weeks, months even, refusing to leave her room. It was up to him to get his younger brother up and ready for school and make sure there was food in the cupboards. He didn't know how to be the head of the household; he wasn't sure his dad had done a particularly good job, even when he was around.

At first, he just took the odd tablet from the medicine cupboard in the bathroom. His mum barely knew what day it was, let alone how many pills she had taken. Luke sold them in the school playground. He took more and more to sell after he realised what a lucrative business it could be. He made a small bit of money and saw his mum smile again when he came home and gave her the cash to get food in or put money on the electric metre. When the school rang his mum, she wouldn't hear a word against him. When she finally opened her eyes, it was too late, and his drug dealing was the only thing keeping the roof over their head. He had long moved on from her medicine cabinet and was making a name for himself on the street.

These days, Luke had his own flat, and he continued to pay his mum's bills so she could stay in the house with his younger brother. She still had her difficulties, but he made sure there was food in the fridge and money in her account to go to the bingo with her friends. Now Fiona was gone, he would need to find someone else to clean and keep her company. James, his brother, wasn't likely to step up and help. Luke tried to encourage his brother to make something of himself and find some sort of get up and go or a personality, but he always preferred to be sat behind a computer screen.

Dylan

Dylan sauntered home from school, hands in his pockets. He didn't mind school; it was clean and warm. The teachers were nice to him. Besides, he knew he would get hassle from the social worker if he didn't go. Dylan learned from a young age to pick his battles.

He knew something wasn't right as soon as he opened the door to the building. The door to their flat was open. He rushed past Fiona's flat, the police tape still hanging from the door as a redundant reminder of what happed to its resident.

'Mum! Mum!'

The living room and kitchen were empty. He dropped his schoolbag and pushed open her bedroom door. His mum was curled up on the bed, clutching her dressing gown around her tightly, gazing into space. He ran to her and pulled the duvet up over her, lying next to her, his arms wrapped tightly around her. She let out a sob, and he loosened his grip, fearing he had hurt her by squeezing too hard. She turned to look at him, a tear running down her cheek, her eye swollen and purple, the red blood vibrant where her lip was split, not yet clotting.

'Who did this to you, Mum?'

'It doesn't matter, Dylan. It doesn't matter, everything is okay,' she said.

Some drawers were open with clothes hanging out, the wardrobe doors open, one hanging off the hinge. He ran to his room, seeing the space where his old PlayStation had been, and the shoe box hidden in the bottom of his wardrobe was now empty on the floor. He wanted to get his mum something nice for her birthday with the money he had put aside. It was all gone. He went back to his mum's room and found her standing at the end of the bed, staring at the wall. Dylan said nothing. He gently guided her to the bathroom and sat her on the closed toilet lid while he put a bath running. He didn't understand what had happened, but he knew their things had been taken and his mum was hurt. When she used drugs, he used to look after her and run her a bath, so he did the same now. As the bath ran, he got her methadone from the fridge. She picked it up twice a week now instead of going to the chemist daily. He knew she would want something if she was feeling bad and wanted to make sure she did not start taking drugs again. He watched her balance the measuring cup on the corner of the bath, ready to pour out the sticky green substance, before thinking better of it and drinking all the contents straight from the bottom.

'Mum…!'

'Just leave me alone for a while, Dylan baby. I need to be alone,' she said. He nodded and started tidying the place up.

The phone ringing broke the silence in the flat. He told his gran everything was okay, when really, he wanted her to come and give him a hug. To tell him everything was okay and to make his mum feel better, but his gran and granddad didn't understand. They wouldn't talk to his mum. He agreed to go to their house for tea one-night next week. He had his own room there if he wanted it, but they had so many rules, and his mum wasn't allowed in their house. Dylan wished they could all live together at his gran and granddad's house, but they said they would never forgive his mum. They wouldn't tell him what happened. He never asked his mum. His grandparents had a big house and lots more money than Dylan and his mum; he couldn't understand why they couldn't all live there together.

Dylan crawled into his mum's bed beside her, and she turned and wrapped her arms around him, holding him close. She was warm, and he breathed in the comforting smell of bubble bath. He stayed there all night. When he woke, he heard singing, and she was in the kitchen making breakfast, acting as if nothing had happened. She had makeup on, trying to cover the bruises on her face, but he could see the dark purple shadows. Dylan knew better than to bring up yesterday and fixed a smile on his face as he joined her in the kitchen.

Her

The sun warmed her skin, and she was smiling as she arrived at the zoo with a friend and her daughter, Ella. It was nice to be outside. They made great smoothies in the café at the zoo. She grabbed Ella's hand while her friend had the other, and they swung her up into the air between them. Ella's giggles made her heart contract, and she wanted to wrap her up and keep her a perfect, innocent little girl forever, sheltered from the world and all its darkness.

'What do you want to see first?'

'Unicorns and Llamas!' Ella shouted, jumping up and down.

'I'm not sure there are any unicorns, but we can certainly have a look. Let's find the llamas first'. They stopped for ice creams on the way and bought monkey nuts to throw for some animals later. The picnic areas were thriving with families, and children's laughter echoed around the playground. The ponies were lined up, ready for the pony rides.

'Ella! What would you say if I said you can have a ride on a unicorn?!' One pony had a sparkling pink ribbon woven through its mane; its coat shimmered with glitter and a unicorn horn between its ears. They took their place at the back of the queue. She recognised two little girls ahead of them. Twins. She frowned, looking around, trying to see a parent so she could place them. There was a man at the edge of the picnic area watching the queue intently. Her hair stood on end, and she rubbed her arms at the sudden chill. She shifted her position, shielding Ella, suddenly hyperaware of their surroundings. She looked again, and his shoulders dropped, his body losing its intensity as someone came up behind him and handed him a bottle of water. As Marie handed him the drink, she gasped in recognition. He put his arm around Marie, and they watched the girls together like any other parents. He wasn't their dad, though, and something didn't feel right.

There was no one ahead of them in the queue now, and Ella was being given a hat and shown how to hold the reins on her unicorn ride.

'Make sure you take pictures of me!' Ella shouted, her eyes shining atop the unicorn.

She smiled at Ella, waving her phone and snapping some pictures. She took a photo with him in the background. Marie gazed up at him, her face beaming. Everyone knew what a shitty husband Carl was, but it couldn't have been a month since he died.

Frank

Frank was starting to look forward to the group. Hearing what others said reassured him that his life wasn't so bad. There was no group today, no job centre to visit, and The Barbican was bathed in sunshine. He headed to the pub for a fry-up and a few pints in the beer garden. He savoured the taste of his beer as he pushed his empty plate away from him, when he heard the click of a lighter at the next table. Frank hadn't smoked for years – he used to before he was married, but she soon put a stop to that. Frank breathed in the smoke as it danced towards him in the breeze, flooding him with nostalgic memories. Memories of being carefree - before his bossy wife, before the black cloud, before the girl's face hit his windscreen, before the noisy jail cell.

'Don't suppose you have a spare one of those?'

She wore a thick layer of makeup, but bruises were peeking through. Frank saw the sadness in her eyes. She eyed him with caution but threw him the packet. He sighed and closed his eyes as he welcomed the hit from the first drag of the cigarette.

'Ex-smoker?'

He nodded as he stood to pass the pack back, swaying, unused to the nicotine on top of too many pints.

'Steady there,' she winced as she leapt up to sit him back down. 'Can I get you a glass of water?'

'No, no, I'm fine, just out of practice,' he waved the cigarette, smiling sheepishly and catching the eye of a passing waitress. 'Another pint when you are ready, please love, and a glass of whatever this lady is having.' The waitress nodded, returning swiftly with their drinks. They made small talk before falling into a companionable silence. He wanted to ask her out, ask her name, ask everything about her. His tongue stuck in his mouth, and his stomach fluttered. Before he could say anything, she finished her wine and stood to leave with a grateful smile.

'Wait,' he burst out as she turned. 'I don't even know your name; can I see you again?'

She smiled softly. 'Same time tomorrow?' He nodded. And so, a new routine began.

That night, Frank was keen to go to bed, so morning would come sooner. She wasn't much of a looker, not bad looking, but nothing like his ex-wife. She wore too much makeup and smoked. She drank in the morning and had an air about her that his mum would say not to get involved with. Despite all this, Frank felt understood. He felt seen.

Morning came, and Frank splashed a little more aftershave on than usual. He shaved and ran some gel through his hair. His mum was beaming at him and said how proud she was that he was making a go of things and making an effort with the job hunting. She handed him his briefcase. He looked at it, a reminder that he should go to the library or the job centre. One day off wouldn't do any harm.

The Professionals

Emma was confused. One minute she and Tom were meeting up regularly at lunch time, and suddenly, he kept making excuses – he had to work, or he had an appointment. Emma was not a chaser; it was usually her who gave the 'it's not you, it's me' speech. She texted Katie and Beth, arranging to meet for lunch and girl talk later at an independent café halfway between the station and Social Services. Lunch time came quickly, and she hovered by Beth's desk, waiting for her to finish her phone call.

'What's happening with you and Tom, anyway?'

'Ugh, don't go there. I think I am being dumped.'

'Ah, you don't need him. What about singles nights?'

Emma blew a raspberry at this suggestion. Katie was already in the café when they arrived and thrust menus at them.

'I'm ravenous. Order first, say hello second,' she smiled. They ordered paninis and various frothy coffees.

'So, what's the crack with Tom?' Emma jumped straight in, trying to glean information from Katie.

'Leave me out of it,' Katie begged. 'Toms neanderthal ways are nothing to do with me'.

'Have you and him ever….'

'God, no.'

'You must have thought about it.'

'Never. He's married for a start. No offence. He's a good mate, but he is a player and will get himself in trouble one of these days.'

'He told me he and his wife are separating.'

'He says a lot of things,' Katie said firmly.

Beth and Emma exchanged glances. The atmosphere was broken as the waitress arrived with their food.

'Anyway,' said Beth, 'who's baking what for the Macmillan coffee morning next month?'

Emma groaned. Beth always got so carried away planning her baking weeks in advance. The Social Services building usually ended up being a bit of a hub for Macmillan mornings. It was central, and usually, their colleagues from other services also baked to contribute. People turned up throughout the day, grazing and buying bits for lunch to take to their own offices. Emma wasn't much of a baker, usually picking up a tray bake from the supermarket on the way in. She could whip up some treats if she put her mind to it, but she didn't see the point when she could get a cake from the shop and avoid the washing up.

~

Kylie met Grace and Anna from Probation, and Sally from Revive for breakfast before work. They all figured they could get away with a slightly late start under the guise of networking.

'Not long now, girls,' said Kylie. The Half Marathon was coming up, and they had formed a little running squad. The girls at work never did ask Kylie, and she decided she wasn't that bothered, anyway. Well, most days she wasn't that bothered. She still had the occasional pang of jealousy when she saw group photos on Facebook or heard them making plans without her. Kylie and Grace ordered a fry-up, Anna had some sort of healthy-looking avocado dish, and Sally went for a bacon sandwich. It was a nice day, although a little chilly, so they sat inside.

'Anyway, Sally, what happened with that man you were seeing?' Kylie asked.

Sally blushed. 'I don't think he is interested in meeting me again,' she said, looking down.

'Oh mate, I'm sorry! We should have a night out,' Kylie declared, keen to cement their friendship beyond work and running. 'Let's get a date in the diary. I'll email you all some suggestions later.'

Grace looked to Anna for approval before agreeing. Kylie couldn't figure those two out. Grace was so lovely but didn't have any confidence. They were an odd match, but their friendship seemed to work. As the foursome left the pub, Kylie nudged Anna nodding towards the outside seating area. They saw Frank at a table, a half-full pint glass in front of him. He was not alone, but a pillar obscured the view of whoever he was with.

Anna sighed, 'We can't win them all.'

'After what he did to those girls, though, that should be enough to stop him drinking for life,' said Grace, uncharacteristically.

'I'll mention it at his next appointment if he doesn't bring it up in group,' Anna replied. Kylie tried to get a glimpse of his companion, but the waitress was in the way.

~

Things were going well for Tom. Since distancing himself from Emma, he had been trying to make more effort at home. He loved his wife; he just missed the excitement, the spontaneity. He wanted to spend time in bed as husband and wife, without lying on a children's toy or being interrupted by the baby monitor. Things had changed, and he supposed he would just have to get used to it. Tom was working at Phoenix today and told himself that just because he promised he would be faithful, that didn't mean he couldn't look and have a flirt.

There were so many nice girls in the agencies he worked with. Probation and addiction services seemed to have a steady stream of girls straight from university working there, a fresh-faced air of innocence about them. For some reason, not many men seemed to apply for the jobs. Revive only employed women so they could provide a safe space for vulnerable women to access support. There was a mixture of the girls like Sally, who were alright, and then the man-hating older women who had been in poor relationships and condemned men forevermore. Those women did his head in and always seemed determined that men could do nothing right. They were so hard to work with and eyed him with suspicion in any meetings or if he dropped anyone off there. He felt like they saw him as someone women needed saving from, and it made him uncomfortable.

~

Beth arrived back to the office, dropping her bag on the desk with a thud.

'Will they ever learn?' she ranted to no one in particular. Emma made a cup of tea while Beth settled and brought it over with a couple of hobnobs. 'Dylan's mum is drinking,' Beth said by explanation.

'I thought she was on a script?'

'She is, but she smelled of alcohol when I was there. Maybe it was a one-off, but I am going to have to keep an eye on things. The poor lad already has a hard enough time without her substituting one addiction for another. I'll give Sally at Revive a call later and see if she has noticed any changes recently.'

'Ah, mate; you are getting them all at the moment. How is the new one you got given? The one who's mum killed herself?'

'Yeh, Katie was pretty messed up about that one.'

'The girl is doing okay, actually. She is still in a kin placement with an aunt for now, but not sure how long that will be sustainable as they don't really have the space. There is a lot of work ahead to figure out if there is anywhere else she can go or if the aunt wants to uproot her own life enough to fight for her.'

Her

She dropped her keys and phone on the worktop, threw her gym kit straight in the washing machine, then frowned, noticing a few dead heads on her lily plant. She carefully snipped them off with the kitchen scissors and headed for the shower. As she closed her eyes and felt the water washing the sweat away, she thought back over her week. She had a satisfying few days closing several files on her caseload at work, taking away some of the pressure, and this put her in a good mood for the weekend. *That was the trouble in this world; no one cared about the people doing the caring. All they wanted was more work in less time, with good statistics to show for it. This seemed the same with her colleagues across the board – police, prison, probation, Social Services and all the supporting agencies. It was all the same.* She saw so many of her colleagues off with stress lately. That reminded her she must check on her friend Jenna. She had been off for a few months now. They usually checked in every few days by text, but she hadn't had a response to her last couple of messages. *If these pathetic addicts would get some sort of grip and stop committing crime there wouldn't be the need for the high caseloads. Therefore, Jenna wouldn't have ended up overworked and eventually off sick with stress.* She didn't mind the ones that drank themselves silly on their own time, in their own homes, funded by their own work or inheritances. *Yes, addicts who minded their own business and didn't bother anyone could crack on. The others were the ones the world could do without.* She hadn't been as on top of monitoring things on the street as much lately; she must keep her head in the game. Tinder had distracted her. Truth be told, Tinder gave her a bit of a buzz at the control and feeling of power when she swiped yes or no, deciding their fate. She knew they would all be swiping yes to her profile.

As the conditioner worked its magic on her hair, her thoughts drifted to her mother. Her mother and Jenna were very much alike – two of life's poor copers. They both struggled with the demons in their heads. Her mother had also struggled to get support for her depression due to the long waiting list and not being a priority. You had to be a crackhead to get priority. If you weren't causing society any problems, you stayed at the bottom of the list. Smash a few windows, rob a granny and get yourself a probation officer – suddenly, referrals were available, and waiting lists magically dispersed.

She stepped out of the shower and looked at herself in the mirror, admiring her curves. She worked hard at the gym, and it was paying off. She had another date tonight. If he played his cards right, this might be the night she invited him back. He was picking her up at 7 pm, and they were going for food at a new Italian restaurant that had opened in town. She quite liked him, and he provided a welcome distraction in the evenings.

Luke

Tilly asked Luke if he could get some MDMA for her and her friends for the weekend. He felt uncomfortable. Even though she knew what he did, they never discussed it, and it was a world that he tried to keep separate from her. He liked Tilly a lot, and her rich girl quirks amused him. He didn't like her taking drugs. He saw what they did to people. The irony wasn't lost on him, but the way he saw it, he had a living to make, and if he didn't supply the drugs, someone else would. It was just business. Drugs were a mug's game, and he had never been stupid enough to take them. He knew Tilly and her friends took drugs when they went out; they said it was only recreational, and it would be better if they got the drugs from him than someone else. Decision eventually made; he sent Tilly a text saying he would give her the powder in time for the weekend.

In the meantime, he had heard word on the street that one of the working girls had been holding back on declaring her earnings. He took a cut in return for protection, and he couldn't be seen to be mugged off this way. He wanted to pay her a visit but was waiting until when she would be out with the other girls. It was a situation that needed to be handled publicly so the others could see they wouldn't get away with it.

'What are you after, boss?'

Luke had already considered this; he didn't want her marked badly enough that it would affect business. Many punters didn't care, but it wasn't a good look having the women out there with bruises on their faces.

'Couple of broken fingers should do it. Stick to one hand so she still has one wrist to make use of. Don't want her completely out of action. It won't hurt the others to see her take a few blows as well – just leave her face alone.' As they arrived at Docker Street, where the girls touted for business, the mood changed. The girls went quiet and disappeared into the shadows. He called Bernie over.

'Anything you want to tell me?'

'No,' she stammered.

'I hear you have been making yourself some extra cash without telling me. You know what happens when I don't get what I'm owed.'

'Please don't, I'll pay you everything, I promise, it was just a misunderstanding. I was always going to give you the money.'

'Too late, you stupid tart,' and Luke walked away, hearing her cry. He cringed. He couldn't show weakness, but he hated the violence towards the women. There was just no other way to keep them in line; they had to know who was boss. It was just business, the same as the drugs. Sometimes Luke thought about getting out of the game, but what else would he do? He snorted to himself at the thought of turning up to an office in a suit and tie. He had to meet Tom quickly to give him a little something he had ordered for the weekend and then planned to pop over to his mum's for a cuppa. That was the thing with people, strip away the class system, the jobs and uniform and judgement, and everyone just wanted to feel good. Drugs gave them that. Tom had been a regular customer for a while now – nurses, coppers, they all liked a bit of sniff at the weekend. Drug workers were the worst.

Her

Her second date had gone well, but she was now regretting inviting him back to her place as he had become a bit needy. They had a good evening, and she enjoyed the time after the date. He stayed all night, and they had coffee in the morning, which was nice, but since then…. He seemed to want to treat the relationship like a done deal. He wanted a lot more commitment from this than she was prepared to offer. She had told him she had a lot on at work and wouldn't be around much for the next week, but it didn't seem to deter him.

She still hadn't heard from her colleague, Jenna, who was off sick and planned to head there after work to check on her. When she got there, her knocks at the door went unanswered. She tried the handle and went on in shouting, 'Hello.' Her nose wrinkled at the musty odour. She noted the takeaway containers piled on the coffee table and unopened post stacked on the sideboard. Anna pushed open the bedroom door, seeing Jenna lying in bed, headphones in, watching something on her iPad. She pulled the curtains open, the light flooding over the bed, making her friend look up in surprise.

'Enough's enough. Time to get up.'

'I don't wanna,' was the response she got as she sat on the end of the bed. She hated seeing her friend like this and wanted to help her. She ran the shower and made her way to the living room to tidy up. Once the windows were open, the takeaway boxes cleared, and the dishes washed and put away, things looked much better. Jenna was still in the shower, so she ran the vacuum around while waiting. By this time, Jenna had still not appeared, and shower steam was drifting on to the hallway. She went back upstairs to chivvy Jenna along.

'I thought he loved me,' Jenna said, sitting on the bed in a towel.

'Okay, this is a conversation that requires food. I'll order something while you get dressed.' She knew from cleaning up that there wasn't much in the kitchen, so placed an order on Just Eat. Jenna eventually appeared in a dressing gown, hair up in a towel, her face pale, and eyes rimmed with red.

'Come on then, what's been going on.'

The entire story came tumbling out. She was already stressed out with work and found support and comfort in the arms of a colleague. When he called it off, she was just about holding things together. She said it had been all hotels and flowers until he confessed; he was married and said he would never leave his wife, and it had just been a bit of fun. She begged him to make a go of it with her and even said she was happy to keep things as they were with her as the other woman. After it was over, she found out she was pregnant. She tried to contact him and blushed at the memory of a series of drunken calls, shamefully begging and crying down the phone. He eventually stopped answering her calls. She saw the doctor, but before any decisions had to be made, she suffered a miscarriage. Jenna sobbed that she didn't know if he ever even knew. He never acknowledged her messages. Between the grief and the sense of impending doom when she thought about her caseload waiting for her return, Jenna was clearly in no state to return to work.

She slammed her fist into the steering wheel before making the journey home from Jenna's, adrenaline rushing through her veins, her teeth clenched. She had always been a quiet child – preferring to stand back and observe. In school, she watched the other children, saw who got into trouble and who got away with their classroom antics. As she got older, she watched boys pulling girls' skirts up and suggesting kiss chase. Again, she watched. Men would approach her mother when they were out together, and she would see her mother flutter her eyelashes, put her hand on their arm and gently turn them down. Her mother would swing her around or link arms conspiratorially, saying there was no room for anyone but them. Until there was. Things changed when her mother had a boyfriend. He lasted two years. Her mother stared at him with her beautiful soulful eyes and hung on his every word. He was always at their house; said he couldn't bear to be apart from her. If they went anywhere without him, he rang to ask what time they would be back. Her mother was different when she had a boyfriend. When he left to live with her best friend, they didn't see either of them again. Her mother became ill. She promised herself that she would always be a better friend than her mother's, and that her happiness would never depend on a man.

The Professionals

Tom and Katie were both on shift when the call came on Saturday night. A teenager overdosed at a local nightclub, Fuel. All spare units were requested to assist. They got there as the paramedics were loading the girl into the ambulance and saw what they assumed to be her three friends standing by the ambulance crying. Tom searched for the manager of the club while Katie approached the girls to see what information she could glean. They saw other uniform staff already carrying out searches as instructed. Katie recognised one girl - she had seen her hanging around with a local dealer, Luke.

The girls were either too drunk or high to make much sense, so the most sensible thing seemed to be to get hold of the parents and get them all home. Hopefully, their friend would be okay, but they would likely all need to be spoken to tomorrow. She left the girls and went to update Tom and the other officers. The girls had confessed they were all underage, so the venue was going to have some serious questions coming their way. Katie looked over as the ambulance pulled away and saw the girls huddled together, speaking in hushed whispers.

'Come on then, girls, time to get you all home to your parents,' Katie said.

'My dad is on the way,' one girl said, so Katie spoke with a colleague who was going to keep an eye on her until he arrived. Katie took the other two girls, Tilly and Deborah. She arrived at Deborah's house first, explaining briefly to her parents that their friend had been taken to hospital and Deborah appeared under the influence. Whatever they had taken seemed to be wearing off now, but Katie advised the parents what to keep an eye out for and not to hesitate to take her to hospital if they were worried. She gave them her card and headed for Tilly's house.

Tilly had clearly not thought to forewarn her parents of the police escort home like Deborah had, and the house was in darkness. After persistent ringing and knocking, Tilly's mum came to the door in a skimpy dressing gown and eye mask pulled up over her hair. She looked from Tilly to Katie and opened the door further to let them in. Katie went through the same information she had with Deborah's parents and said she would be in touch. Tilly's mum was furious, demanding to know who had given them drugs. Katie kept her suspicions to herself.

Katie radioed control to check if she was needed back at Fuel and was informed things were under control. Tom had texted her, saying he would get a lift with another patrol vehicle, so she headed back to the station to start on the paperwork. Tom soon joined her, and with an update from the hospital. The girl was in a critical condition; her parents were there and were being prepared for the worst. Even though his daughter was only a baby, Tom wanted to rush home, hold her close and never let go. He resisted the urge to ring his wife. He was still on best behaviour, and he didn't think ringing in the middle of the night to FaceTime their sleeping daughter would go down well.

Paperwork partially complete, they received another call. When they arrived at the 24hr Spar shop, they found Frank drunkenly trying to purchase more alcohol.

'Bloody typical,' slurred Frank. 'it's always you,' he pointed his finger at Tom.

'For fuck's sake, Frank, I thought you were past this. Come on, let's get you home to your mum.'

'I'm not going. I just want to buy a bottle of whiskey, and I'll be on my way,' he said haughtily. Another 10 minutes of reasoning and Frank gave in and allowed them to give him a lift home. Tom had seen how much Frank's mum had been through already and hated seeing what Frank was putting her through again.

'Did you learn nothing from the crash and your time in prison? What about the course?' Tom attempted to reason with Frank. Frank just folded his arms, sulking and occasionally muttering to himself. They should have taken him to the cells, really, but they knew that would be another thing for his mum to worry about. At least this way, she knew he was home safely.

Frank

When Frank had sobered up and slept off his escapades, he came downstairs to find his mum sitting at the kitchen table sobbing. The sight of this same scene he saw far too often caused shame to wash over him. She asked him the questions she always asked. 'What did I do wrong? Is your life so awful that you must keep getting yourself in this state? When did I lose you?' Frank felt his heart sink. He moved to comfort her, and she turned into him, allowing him to envelope her in a bear hug. He was already nauseous; a combination of shame and a hangover, and his mum's perfume made it worse. Even when she wasn't leaving the house, she always did her hair and makeup, dressed nicely and finished with a spritz of Anais Anais.

Frank hadn't planned to stay out on the booze last night, it just happened. It always 'just happened'. He had an appointment with probation on Monday, and he knew he was going to get nagged when they got wind of what had happened. Frank had always been a staunch rule follower; he hated the thought of being in trouble.

When Frank arrived at his appointment with Anna and was shown to an interview room, Kylie from Phoenix was waiting. Frank's heart sank, and he knew Tom had told them about the weekend so they could both tell him off.

'Come on through, Frank,' summoned Anna, her face unreadable. They sat around the desk in the interview room. 'Why do you think I've asked Kylie to join us today?'

Frank came clean and told them about Tom taking him home at the weekend after his drunken behaviour. He spoke about his struggles and how he feels he isn't making any progress in moving on with his life. Kylie asked about his support network and if he was seeing anyone. Frank hesitated, confused why she had asked, before deciding it best to deny his burgeoning relationship. They often lectured him on the risks of jumping into a relationship too soon, and he wasn't in the mood for another one. He knew they were just doing their jobs, but this wasn't his life – being dragged in here for what felt like a telling-off. He was a grown man, for god's sake, and he was living with his mum and being told off in probation in a way he could only compare to being back in school and summoned to the headteacher's Office. Only in this case, the headteacher had been replaced with two girls who were at least ten years younger than him.

Frank was saved from answering further questions by the piercing sound of an alarm, followed by shouting and banging coming from another interview room. Moments later, the door opened, and the stressed-looking receptionist said they needed to end the appointment immediately, and staff should return to their desks via the rear stairwell. Frank found himself shown out via the fire exit at the back of the building. Anna and Kylie apologised, clearly with no more idea what was going on than he had. They said they would be in touch but encouraged him to talk about his drinking at the weekend in the group at Phoenix tomorrow. Appointment cut short; Frank pottered off to the pub to see if his new friend was there.

Everyone was in attendance for the group the next day, with Kylie and Tom leading the session. Frank knew he couldn't

114

avoid talking about his weekend, and he resigned himself to owning up and taking whatever was coming his way. He started with an apology to Tom, his cheeks flushed with shame. Whilst he got on with the others in the group, he couldn't help but feel bitter that he was sitting in a room among drug addicts and thugs, yet he was the one apologising for his behaviour. They spent some time talking about the potential consequences of Frank drinking again, and his peers offered him tips and ideas to help him avoid a repeat of this situation. 'Peers.' Frank didn't see them as peers. He wouldn't say he saw himself as above them, he just never quite accepted his new place in society. Talk moved on to another lad in the group who had had issues this week as his dad was home from the military, which always made his home life more volatile. The street workers were quiet. One of them, Bernie, was clearly in pain. She had a bandage on one of her hands, and Frank couldn't help noticing her wince as she moved. Still being a Gentleman at heart, he found himself making a drink for her in the break. She was easy to talk to, and he told her about his budding new relationship. It felt nice to have someone to confide in. He also took some comfort that no matter how shit he felt his life was, at least he was in a better position than Bernie.

The
Professionals

Kylie and Tom hadn't much chance to talk before the group but agreed to put some time aside after to have a catch up on how things were going. They agreed Frank was not being honest with any of them, but there was little they could do until he was ready to open up.

'Anna and I tried to have a meeting with him at Probation yesterday,' Kylie shared, 'but the alarm bell cut it short.'

'I heard about that; assaulted a newly qualified Probation Officer. Don't know all the details yet, but he was questioned and released until further investigations have taken place. One of the drunks who hangs about in the car park at the bottom of town. The girl was new and is pretty shaken up. She will be okay physically, a bit of bruising and banged her head on the wall.'

'Shit,' said Kylie, visibly shaken, 'hopefully they charge him when they see the CCTV.'

'If the cameras were working,' said Tom. With budget cuts across the board, they both knew that many of the cameras around the city had stopped working over the years and hadn't been a priority to repair. They discussed the other members of the group with no major concerns except to monitor Bernie, the prostitute. No-one was really clear about what happened to her, as she remained tight-lipped, but she was clearly in a lot of pain. Tom had heard a whisper that she owed money, so they hoped this would be the end of it. Part of the job involved knowing when to get involved and when the rules of the street needed to be allowed to play out. Bernie wasn't seriously injured, and hopefully, she had learned her lesson, and there would be no more trouble. Sadly, unless she asked for help or gave a name, which would never happen, there was very little that they could do.

Back at her desk, Kylie emailed the staff involved in the group with updates. As Tom left the centre, he saw Luke outside and took the opportunity to ask him about Bernie. 'All sorted, Boss,' said Luke, 'there shouldn't be any more trouble.' Tom gave a nod of understanding.

~

Beth was filling Emma in on her day over a hot chocolate. She had received a call from Sally at Revive about Dylan's Mum, who she suspected was drinking.

'I meant to call her, but she beat me to it, and it looks like I was right. Sally thinks she has been drinking as well. It's hard because technically, her issue is with drugs, but I am worried she will switch one addiction for another.'

'Has she said anything about it to you?'

'No, I plan to ask her about it at her next review, but if she doesn't smell of drink and there is no evidence to suggest a problem or risk to Dylan, there is not a lot I can do aside from continue to monitor the situation. The other thing Sally said I need to discuss with her is that she has apparently met some new bloke. This isn't one of her paying clients, but apparently, she hasn't told this poor man what she does for a living.'

Emma laughed, 'Can you imagine finding out your girlfriend is a hooker?' she said a bit too loudly, lowering her voice when she saw the older women at the next table looking over disapprovingly. 'I suppose at least that means he doesn't have to pay like the others.'

Beth cut the muffin between them and pushed half towards Emma as Emma said she was thinking about signing up for a Speed Dating event at Royal William Yard. Whilst Beth loved hearing about Emma's escapades and dating tales, she was glad that she was happily married and didn't have to put herself out there in that way. She didn't have the confidence Emma had, and dating seemed much more complicated than years ago when she met her husband.

~

Katie was on the late shift catching up on paperwork at the station. She saw in the local newspaper that Leanne, the girl who was taken to hospital at the weekend, had died from a suspected drug overdose. She hung on for a couple of days whilst the doctors did their best to save her, but it was too late. Her young body gave up fighting. Katie had been on a rest day on Monday, so hadn't been in the station for the official updates. As she loaded up the file on the computer, she saw several entries and ongoing lines of enquiry. It took some time to get access to Leanne's phone - iPhones were such a pain if you didn't have the password. They eventually downloaded the data with little -interest. It looked like the other girls on the night out with her were the ones planning to take drugs, and this poor Leanne girl was usually the one who didn't join in. 'What was different this time?' asked Katie, looking at Leanne's face smiling back at her from the photo her parents had provided. It was clear from the friend's WhatsApp group that, as usual, Leanne didn't intend to take anything despite peer pressure and goading from the others. There had been no activity in the group since Friday night, so they had clearly been communicating by other means or started a new group. Katie could see that Leanne's parents had been assigned a Family Liaison Officer. The FLO would support them through the next steps of the enquiry, help with managing the press interest and signpost additional support and counselling services should they need it.

There was no mention of Luke in the file, but Katie had seen him and Tilly together a few times and suspected that he was the boyfriend Tilly referred to in her messages to her friends. If this was the case, it was likely that Luke supplied them with the drugs. Katie had been tasked with following up with Tilly and her mother, having already met them on the night. She checked her watch, 7 pm, not too late to call them and see if she could pop over.

Luke

Luke was missing Tilly. He was also worried about what she might say to the police. A school friend of hers slipped a note to him yesterday saying that her mum had taken her phone away from her and grounded her. Not to be outfoxed by Tilly's mum, he had put a new burner phone in an envelope and had bribed his younger brother to try to pass it to her at the school gate. The teachers were loitering more than usual and had been tasked with keeping the students from sneaking out. Luke's brother, James, was young enough to blend in near the school gates. Luke wished he could get his brother out and about in the real world more. He was always shut away in his bedroom, and Luke had never heard him mention a girlfriend or a boyfriend, for that matter. It had taken a good wad of cash to convince James to leave his room and do Luke a favour. Of course, there were other people he could have got to do it for free, but he kept meaning to try and encourage James to get out more, and this was a good opportunity. His mum didn't seem too bothered and just gave the excuse that everyone was different and that we all have our own interests. Luke thought she just enjoyed having him there to cook for and look after. He would soon finish his college course in IT and would need to get out and find a job. He would have a chat with James next time he was there. Maybe he should suggest a family meal to his mum; she'd love an excuse to cook for her boys.

Luke thought he must find someone else to help her out around the house. He still felt guilty for what happened to Bernie after her stealing. He knew from her takings that she would be short of money since his act of retribution. He sighed. Why did they put him in that position time and time again? Luke decided he would offer the cleaning work to her on a trial basis; she wasn't a bad sort, just made some silly decisions. He'd make it clear that there were to be no drugs in the house, and he felt sure she was aware of the consequences if she even thought about stealing or trying to rip him off again.

Luke's phone rang. It showed the number of the burner phone James had passed to Tilly. He smiled and answered it.

'I haven't got long,' Tilly whispered over the sound of running water. She explained that she was still grounded until she told her mum where the drugs came from. She told him about the visit from Katie earlier that evening and that she had told everyone Leanne must have bought the drugs herself in the club. The other girls would stick to the story as Leanne never took drugs with them and had, as usual, declined when offered. Luke wondered who the girl had got the drugs from, if not Tilly. He knew some of his boys had been out Friday night and planned to ask around to check for a trail that led back to him. What with Fiona's death recently and now this underage girl, there was going to be a spotlight on the dealers for a few weeks. He would make sure they stayed under the radar until things blew over. Aside from that, he liked to know who else was dealing on his turf to make sure he got his cut.

Her

She was still furious that the alcoholic waster had been allowed back out on the streets after what he did to the new Probation Officer. *How dare he think he could get away with it? How dare the system let him get away with it?* She heard he pushed the poor girl up against a wall in an interview room, shaking her by the arm. They were all expected to put up with this sort of behaviour these days. A friend had been spat at only the other day, and other than a note in the offenders file and a shoulder shrug from management, nothing would be done. It was the same across the board – police, probation, prison, Social Services, everyone was in the same boat. *When would the hierarchy make offenders accountable for their actions?* Poor Jenna was still off work, though it looked like a phased return might be on the cards soon. There were so many genuine people that would be worthy of the extra time with them. People who demonstrated remorse, people who wanted to change and live a life worth living. When they worked with so many different people, day in, day out, how were they ever supposed to do any meaningful work?

She needed to run. She tied her laces and slammed the door on the way out, feeling irritated. Usually, with each strike of her feet on the pavement, she would feel her cares and worries falling away from her. The fresh air and the freedom running gave her usually lifted her mood on even the worst of days. Today was different; something stopped the cloud from lifting. She followed one of her regular routes, towards the bottom of town, past the flats and the car park. She felt her annoyance boiling under the surface as she saw the rabble gathered in the car park as if they were a normal group of people socialising rather than addicts draining all they could from the system. The offender who assaulted the Probation Officer was there. He was smoking and laughing without a care in the world. They hadn't been able to hold him in custody, and he'd been released pending investigation. What a joke. A seed of an idea began to formulate in her mind, a way she might take out a few of these scumbags in one go – it was risky, but it might be interesting. Her thoughts bounced from poison, to chemical, to plant. Her brain, a well-oiled machine weighing up her options, mentally scanning each idea for availability, traceability. She bounced back to the reasons why she was even considering this - her motivation, the people that would have access to support and community resources if these people were no longer wasting funding. It was a question of sacrifice. She was saving these people from themselves – their own inevitable downfall, and in the meantime, this sacrifice allowed others to have their chance to flourish.

She kept running along Docker Street, keeping her head down when she saw Bernie with the other women. The working girls didn't generally cause too many problems. They turned up in the group now and then, like Bernie, and occasionally made their way through the justice system, but most skated by under the radar. They had people like Luke, who ruled their world but also kept them topped up on drugs so they didn't turn to crime to get them.

Now that she had her next project, she felt better as she looped back through the city centre and jogged in the direction of home. She watered her plants and sent a quick text to check their meeting time for the Half Marathon. She hadn't intended to run as far as she had, but she was fuelled by injustice.

The Professionals

It appeared everyone was at the Half Marathon. Several staff across the services had signed up for the event, raising money for various charities. The staff from Revive were in matching brightly coloured t-shirts carrying buckets for their cause. The probation and police staff seemed a bit more incognito in their usual running gear, though a couple wore t-shirts raising awareness for their chosen charities. Tom and a few of his fellow male officers were dressed as lifeguards from Baywatch. They tried, unsuccessfully, to get some of the women to join them with their chosen theme. Katie left them preening to chat with Kylie, who looked like she was waiting for her running pals to arrive. She spotted Beth and Emma and gave them a wave. There was an excellent turnout for the event, and everyone was in good spirits. The city turned out well as a community for the yearly event, and the crowds would soon line the roads to cheer on the runners.

Beth and Emma ran together regularly and quickly settled into a steady pace. Now and then, one of them would comment on someone in the crowd or express displeasure at a hill.

'Why do people think it is okay to stand in the crowds cheering whilst blowing smoke into our path?' huffed Emma. It was annoying how many people did this, oblivious to others. Whilst the city was big, whenever events like this happened, it felt as though everyone you knew was there. The route pushed the runners through the City Centre, past the flats at the bottom of town and back along Plymouth Hoe with beautiful sea views to finish. Emma and Beth fell silent as they picked up the pace for the last part of the run. They followed the runners ahead of them along the cobbled streets of The Barbican past the pubs and beer gardens. Some customers in the pubs would give the odd clap or whoop of encouragement at the runners. Neither Beth nor Emma commented at the time, but they both noticed the familiar couple sitting and enjoying each other's company, a table full of empty glasses between them. As they ran through the finishing arch, they saw Katie ahead, accepting her medal and banana.

'I don't know who wants a banana,' Emma puffed, 'I want a Mars bar or a plate of chips presented to me for my efforts, not a bloody banana.' Tom finished a while before them and was posing again, this time with a group of volunteers for photos. Emma couldn't help running her eyes over those abs. Her mind told her no, but her body was not ready to let him go.

'Once a cheat, always a cheat. What is it they say? When the mistress becomes the wife, there is a vacancy for a new mistress,' said Beth steering her friend in the opposite direction. 'Fancy an ice cream while I tell you which of my clients I saw getting pissed?'

'Always. I also spotted one outside the pub, one bloke from my group.'

Ice creams in hand, they kept moving to stop their muscles seizing up from the build- up of lactic acid. They frequently

126

passed other runners enjoying the nice weather with their families post-run and exchanged conspiratorial nods and affirmations. They discovered that the client Beth mentioned previously was sat drinking with the group Emma had referred to.

Luke

Luke and Tilly had devised a way to see each other – her mum said she could still run the Half Marathon, even though she was technically still grounded. She was going to sneak off so they would have an hour or so together, and she would then reappear at the finish line. Her mum had gone off shopping, so wouldn't be waiting along the route with other friends, parents, partners, and well-wishers. Luke was still confused about who had given her friend the drugs and wanted to assure Tilly that he would get to the bottom of it for her. Her eyes welled up as he mentioned Leanne, and she said the funeral was being arranged for the week after next. She looked like she was going to say something else but stopped and changed the subject abruptly. Luke didn't push her on it.

Tilly's 18th birthday was coming up in the next couple of weeks, and she asked what he was planning for her. Luke was planning to whisk her away to a nice spa hotel in Newquay for a weekend, but with her being grounded, he would have to think of something else. He reluctantly said goodbye to Tilly so she could sneak back in and cross the finish line. Luke saw a topless Tom in red shorts getting in a car with someone wearing a volunteer t-shirt. He would have to remember to give the guy some stick for using the run to pick up women. He shook his head, grinning, and headed off to meet Bernie.

Bernie's hand was no longer bandaged, but two of her fingers were splinted together, still showing colourful bruising. Luke was taking her to meet his mum and let her know the expectations of the cleaning job. He sent his mum a text to say they were on the way, and she had made a pot of tea by the time they arrived. He noted she had tidied up the place and put some makeup on. She always liked to make a good first impression did his old mum. Little did she know she was sprucing herself up for a prostitute. She knew some of his business dealings were not a mother's first choice for her son, but she looked the other way. He knew she knew about the drugs, but she had never mentioned the hookers. She must be aware as people talked, but it wasn't a conversation he thought they needed to have. Jackie was happy to pretend she knew nothing, to take the money Luke gave her, and he was happy to pretend he was still her innocent little boy. To be fair to Bernie, she had tarted herself up less than usual and was wearing jeans and a jacket. He had never seen her with so little flesh on show. He went upstairs to see if James was home while his mum showed Bernie around. As usual, James was holed up in his room like a teenager. As Luke opened the door, he smirked as whatever James was doing disappeared as he turned the screen off. He swivelled his chair around to Luke, giving him grief about knocking.

'Caught you watching porn, did I?' Luke teased. James went bright red as he denied it. Bernie and his mum appeared, and Luke introduced Bernie to James, who said that his room was off-limits. Bernie nodded in acknowledgement, peering over his shoulder at the two large computer screens and other expensive-looking equipment.

Cups of tea drained, job discussed, and all necessary introductions made, Luke offered to drop Bernie back to town, giving her a small bag of white powder. She accepted it with a nod.

Her

What was Frank playing at? What on earth was he doing in a relationship with her? The pair of them should know better. Neither of them should be drinking, let alone in the middle of the day. Where was her son? Where was Franks remorse? She had been stewing on this since seeing them together on the day of the Half Marathon. These oblivious individuals must be stopped before they hurt more people. A sacrifice must be made, because they clearly weren't going to put anyone else before their own selfish needs. Frank was already on thin ice with her because of his drinking again. She dressed in her usual dark clothing, blending in with the shadows, and made her way towards the flats. She hovered outside, watching the door. She couldn't risk going into the building, not knowing who would be in the flat. She smiled to herself as she imagined the looks on their faces if she burst in and caught them in the act. She shook her head to get rid of the image, both amused and repulsed. Bingo! she thought as she saw Frank coming out of the building, but where was the boy? She edged closer. She patted the bottle of drugged vodka in her bag. Valium was easier to get hold of than a decent cocktail these days. Just then, she saw the boy return. She kept watch, thinking she would have to try again another night, but a few minutes later, he came back out of the flat, scurrying off around the corner.

This was her moment. She quickly edged towards the building and slipped in the unlocked front door towards Dylan's mum's flat. The faint sound of music drifting into the hallway sounded like it might be coming from the bedroom. She knew from being in Fiona's flat that there would be a small hallway just inside the door. She pulled her cap lower, ensuring her face was obscured, as she tilted her head down and tried the flat door. The music was a little louder now, definitely coming from one of the bedrooms. She slipped into the kitchen, taking a glass from the draining board, and emptied the drugged vodka into the glass. Sadly, she wouldn't be around to see this one. She would have preferred to find a way to get rid of Dylan's mum without him being the one to find her. It wasn't a good experience for the boy, finding his mum dead, but he'd probably seen and experienced far more than he should already. It was a means to an end, and he would have a chance at a better future with her gone. Given that she was already a known addict and had been seen drinking, hopefully, this one would be ruled an overdose with no questions asked. It helped that Fiona had overdosed in the building recently, as the investigators would tie it all up neatly as a rough area with high rates of drug use. Vodka laced with Valium was the perfect combination for her last drink. Of course, if she were to suddenly see the light and prove herself to be a worthy parent by not drinking the vodka, she would survive. This could be seen as a test!

The Professionals

Some days, Katie didn't enjoy her job. She heard over the radio, when she was on the way to Beth's office, that an unresponsive female had been found in the flats at the bottom of town but hadn't connected the dots until Beth got the call. Dylan's mum was found dead - overdose by the sound of it. Beth's heart broke for Dylan. Despite all the shitty things she did as a mother, that boy idolised her. The officers told Beth he found her this morning and tried to wake her before calling 999. When Beth and Katie arrived at the flats, there were already police cars and tape everywhere. There was a stretcher outside waiting to be given the all clear to retrieve her body. Katie vouched for Beth to the officers at the cordon, and they ducked under the tape, making their way to the communal entrance. Beth saw Dylan hunched up, his knees tight to his chest, sitting on the pavement.

'I'll find out what's happening and come back to you,' Katie assured her, leaving Beth to go to Dylan. The officer by his side looked relieved at being able to get away from the troubled boy. Beth said nothing, just sat down beside him.

Eventually, he spoke, 'What will happen to me?' Beth thought of her own children and hoped they never had to go through something so awful. She handed him a tissue and said she would take him back to her office while they figured some things out. He nodded as Katie reappeared.

'We will need to find out if anyone has spoken to your grandparents yet. I'll be back in a moment,' Beth said, 'I'll be just over there where you can see me. I just need to speak to the officer.'

Katie advised Beth she was okay to take Dylan back to the Social Services office while they planned the next steps. She had been dead for some time, it turned out, probably most of the night. The scene was disturbed where Dylan had tried to wake her, but initial thoughts were drugs and/ or alcohol. They had to wait for toxicology results to get a definite answer, not that it mattered. A young boy had still lost his mum, whatever the outcome. An Officer interrupted them holding a phone. It stopped ringing as he approached, and Dylan lurched towards them.

'That's my mum's. Give it to me. Stop touching her stuff.'

The Officer asked if they knew who Frank was; Beth said she would make sure she passed his details, along with next of kin, to officers so they could let them know.

'I think we need to get Dylan away from here now.'

Back at the office, she left Dylan in the family room while she went to make some calls. She asked Emma to pass on Frank's details to Katie. Emma said she would let Katie and the rest of the addiction group facilitators know so they were ready to support him. She quickly tapped out a group email, marking it as top priority.

Frank

Panic gripped his chest as he opened the door and saw two police officers. Frank racked his brain, trying to remember what he had done. He knew he had been drinking too much again, and some mornings, he struggled to remember much about the night before. His mother appeared by his side, her face filled with worry, as he stepped aside to let the officers in. The officers looked serious and suggested they all sit down.

Frank was devastated. He really thought that meeting her was going to help turn his life around. He finally felt that there might be a chance he could be happy again. Every time he thought things might go his way; something came along to remind him that his life was a mess. He had seen the hurt in his mum's eyes that he hadn't told her he had met someone. She liked to think they shared everything these days. After the officers had left, he had a call from Tom. He had obviously been waiting for them to let him know he had been told. Tom encouraged him to attend the group and to call Kylie or Anna if he needed extra support. All Frank wanted was a drink.

Unfortunately for Frank, or fortunately as everyone else saw it, he had just settled with a pint when Sally walked past the pub. She sat down beside him, her eyes filled with genuine sorrow.

'I heard what happened. I can't imagine what you are going through, but you know this won't help,' she soothed. 'You have group in a minute. Come on, I'll walk with you.' Sally walked him to the door and left him with Bernie, saying she needed to find Tom while she was there. And that is how Frank found himself sitting in a room full of fellow fuck-ups, crying over someone he had only known for a few weeks. They all reassured him, said the right things, and offered platitudes, but it wouldn't bring her back.

The Professionals

'Look at you with a different woman each week,' teased Luke as Tom stood outside the agency with Sally. Sally blushed.

'Men and woman can just be friends, you know,' Tom batted back good-naturedly.

'I saw you with the volunteer at the weekend as well. You will have to give me some tips one day.' Sally looked at Tom questioningly, hurt barely concealed in her eyes. He knew he needed to shake her off. He shouldn't have gone back to her place a second time and didn't know how she would react when he told her it couldn't happen again. All he needed was for her to shout her mouth off to the man-haters at Revive and his precarious reputation would take another knock.

'If you ever get bored of all the wining and dining and want a professional, I'll sort you out a discount,' Luke winked as he stubbed his cigarette out on the wall and flicked the butt in the road.

~

Katie was frustrated. Nothing seemed to turn up with Leanne, the overdosed teenager. The girls had nothing new to say, and nothing further had turned up on Leanne's phone. The CCTV in the club wasn't much help; there was a good view of the exits, but too many blind spots inside the club. There had been none of the regular dealers spotted being in the club at the same time as the girls. If Leanne had refused to take drugs with her friends, who had she got them from? She knew Tom had a bit of an understanding with Luke and texted him asking if he could get any information off the record. If there were someone new dealing, Luke would know. Whether he would give them any information was another matter. She put her phone away and checked her watch. She'd been asked to pop into the probation offices at some point today. Since the assault, they tried to show increased police presence and give a zero-tolerance message. She bypassed the staff entrance she usually used and entered through the main reception, smiling hello to the reception girls on the way through. There wasn't anyone of interest in the waiting room, a couple of shoplifters, a young-looking girl she hadn't seen around before, and an older man. She hadn't met the man but had seen him in the news, having recently been released from prison. A retired Head Teacher, his conviction for historic sex abuse of pupils had been a high-profile one. She had met a few of his victims. It was so sad when they ended up turning to drugs and crime to escape from the memory of whatever horror he subjected them too. It was no wonder though really, when you heard their stories. His family stood by him, choosing not to believe the words of his copious victims. She was heading upstairs for a cup of tea and a natter with Grace and Anna before her shift ended but took the route past the interview rooms so they would all see there was an officer on site if needed.

~

Grace scurried off to make drinks while Anna dragged a chair over for Katie. Katie liked Grace but also didn't quite know what to make of her. She was so quiet and reserved for someone who worked in a job that demanded assertiveness and someone who could hold their own. Maybe she was different with the offenders, a second persona. She often saw how quickly people could change in her line of work. An aggressor might suddenly play the victim to plead their innocence. Equally, she saw people flip as if a switch went off inside them, and a red mist descended. People were fascinating creatures.

Her

The rain held off, and it was a nice day. She was meeting friends in the park later to go for a walk and looked forward to the fresh air and catch up. She put the Tinder dates on hold for the time being and felt a bit more focused on her side projects. She was sad she hadn't been able to see the life drain from Dylan's mum's eyes as she had with Fiona, but the job was done. The newspapers reported the story of a prostitute who died from a cocktail of drink and drugs. There was no mention of the boy. She was glad. His life was screwed up enough already.

As she walked through the park towards the fountain, where they were meeting, she saw a children's birthday party in full swing. Remembering her own birthdays as a child, she smiled at the fond memories. Her mum always went all out for her birthday, even when her boyfriend was living with them. It was the one day that was all about them. She recognised two of the little girls as Marie's children but couldn't see Marie with the other mums who hung back nearby while the children played. She looked around and spotted John. He stood apart from the other parents chatting to a young lad. She didn't recognise the boy; he looked about college age, and she idly wondered what they could have found to talk about. It looked like John handed something to the boy before he walked away. The boy looked around furtively before slipping it into his pocket. Interesting, she thought, as John sauntered over to where the other parents were gathered.

She waved hello to her friends, removing her headphones ready for some girl talk. She was pleased to see Jenna had made it. Jenna was still not back to work, but they all encouraged her to get out and about, and this was a big step in the right direction. Jenna was looking over at the birthday party, a wistful look on her face.

'We could have been so happy,' she said, 'why didn't he want us?'

A tear rolled down her friend's cheek, and she saw her subconsciously put a hand on her stomach, thinking of what might have been. Jenna remained tight-lipped about who 'he' was. She couldn't help but feel it must be someone they knew if Jenna wouldn't divulge any information. She didn't think Jenna would be stupid enough to have a relationship with a client, but the thought had crossed her mind, more than once. She sighed; it was going to be one of those meet-ups. She prepared herself to rally the troops for a pep talk for Jenna. She hated seeing her friends upset like this, especially at the hands of a man. If only she could find out who he was.

The
Professionals

Tom and Phil were heading out to take witness statements following an RTC over the weekend when they got the call asking them to attend a residential address nearby. There were reports of harassment. The house belonged to a recently released retired Head Teacher, Arthur McIntyre and his wife. As they arrived, they saw 'nonce' written across the front door in blood-red spray paint. There was similar graffiti on the garage door. The front door was opened by a nervous-looking older woman, who steered them through to the lounge, where she sat on a sofa clasping her hands together.

'It's starting again,' she said 'it's bad enough that I had to go through all this before, but now he is out it's starting again.'

Tom remembered the case from his early days as a Police Officer. He recalled the wife and daughter being harassed by the local community. They didn't help themselves by standing by him and refusing to accept his offences. Arthur's release, understandably, prompted unease in the local community, who were forced to relive old memories and see his face around town again. There wasn't much Tom or Phil could do other than give their cards to the distraught woman and try to reassure her by saying they would see if the neighbourhood patrol units could drive by a bit more often. Tom noticed pictures of the couple's daughter and grandchildren and made a mental note to check the restrictions around access to his grandchildren. It was all very well his daughter maintaining his innocence when he was in custody, but it would be interesting to see if her stance changed now that she had her own children and he had been released.

~

Beth pulled up outside the double-fronted Edwardian house. She was visiting Dylan to see how things were going living with his grandparents. The house was immaculately presented with neat bushes lining the front garden and colourful borders of flowers. The front door was surrounded by the original ornate stained glass, and she could see the shadow of someone coming towards the door after she pushed the bell. The smell of baking drifted to the porch, making Beth's stomach rumble. It amused her how many people thought freshly baked snacks would keep the Social Workers on their side. Although, to be fair, in this instance, it was probably more of a generational thing, baking for guests.

Dylan's grandmother opened the door smiling and told her to go into the sitting room while she fetched the cake. Beth had been to the house before, but there was so much to take in in the spacious hallway. The original tiled floor was maintained well, and the walls were lined with pictures taken over decades. She saw pictures of Dylan's Mum as a child on the swing she had seen in the rear garden. There were many pictures of her as a child, smiling with her parents. They became fewer as she grew into a teenager. There were photos of Dylan and lots of pictures of his grandparents with their friends. Beth smiled at their wedding photo with the old-fashioned hair styles and beautifully detailed dress. One of the men in the photos stood out, but she couldn't place him. He appeared in photos taken over several years - mostly at dinner and garden parties. Her thoughts were interrupted by Dylan's grandmother, Martha, coming back through and asking her to hold the door open to the sitting room. Beth was served tea and warm cake as Dylan arrived. They discussed how things were going, and Dylan seemed happy to stay with his grandparents. There were no concerns at present, but Beth expressed that there would still need to be a full assessment before this could be considered a permanent place of residence for Dylan. Dylan's grandfather, Brian, could not be there, and Beth arranged to return when she could speak with him as well.

Her

She enjoyed baking and intended to spend the weekend cooking up a storm. There was no exact science to her plan as there was never a guarantee with Lily of the Valley poisoning, but she loved the buzz of not knowing what would happen. Usually, she liked things to be a bit more precise and planned, but this was an experiment and could be extremely useful in the future. She read that the berries and leaves were poisonous to children and animals - the warnings were less severe for adults. She hoped that the already weakened immune systems of the street drinkers and junkies would benefit her. It would be interesting to see how it panned out, and might be something she could refine. Maybe not everyone had to die. Maybe some would learn their lesson from a health scare, a wake-up call. She mulled over the recent euthanasia of unworthy individuals she had executed. There had been no grand plan that this was her thing now, a new hobby, but somehow it was. Like having a part-time job on the side. In fact, Carl's untimely demise had been very much opportunistic. She often thought about getting rid of people over the years, but until Carl hadn't thought she would follow through with it. It just proved sometimes you just have to stop thinking about things and get on with it, and it had been so easy so far. Until now, it had been more of vicarious thought. Normal people didn't go around doing this sort of thing; it wasn't considered an acceptable solution to deal with a very real problem. She had toyed with the idea, entertained the details and imagined what the world might look like if the unworthy were removed.

Many deaths are ruled misdemeanour or left as an open case of unsolved murder. Even with advances in technology, there are so many TV shows these days that make it easier - you can switch on many shows, fictional or true crime and get a thorough understanding of factors to consider - blood spatter, DNA and things most likely to raise questions. Most people know about gunpowder residue and getting rid of blood. Her mind was drifting. Right, back to the task at hand. She had arranged to go out with the rough sleeper's team, who check on the street homeless. They hand out food and drinks and confirm homeless status to the council for those seeking accommodation. She planned to make flapjacks with the berries from her Lily of the Valley plant and would take these along when she went out with them. It was arranged for the night after the MacMillan coffee morning as she knew they would package up any leftovers, so it would be a splendid opportunity to slip her special flapjacks in.

Marie

This was the weekend Marie had been waiting for. She and John hadn't yet cemented their relationship in the bedroom, and she planned a romantic evening without the girls. Marie had dropped the twins off at a school friend's house for a sleepover and shaved her legs and bikini line and fake tanned in preparation. She treated herself to some new underwear and felt good. She marvelled again at how lucky they were to have John in their lives. He was so patient and put no pressure on her to take their relationship further, if anything being too understanding. She wanted to show him she appreciated him and she was all his. When John arrived, she had already had a couple of glasses of wine whilst cooking and was slightly tipsy. She hadn't told him the girls were out, and he seemed a little disappointed it was just the two of them. This only made him more attractive to her - how many men would be so open to dating a woman with two young girls? It wasn't easy to be a father figure to someone else's children. John cleared away the plates after their meal, kissing her on the neck as he leaned over her shoulder to refill her wineglass. 'Steady,' she giggled, 'I'll be too drunk for later.' They enjoyed easy flirtation over chocolates for dessert and moved to the sofa. Marie found herself quite drunk, leaving red splashes on the table where she slopped her wine. She snuggled into John, inhaling his familiar smell, pulling him closer. She hadn't intended to drink so much and felt her head spinning as she closed her eyes for a kiss.

Marie woke up the next morning with a parched mouth and a sore rib where her bra had been digging in overnight. Looked under the cover; she saw she still wore the sexy yet impractical underwear she'd put on yesterday evening. She searched her memory for what had happened last night and remembered stumbling to the sofa after dinner. She couldn't remember going to bed, but there was a glass of water on the bedside table, and she could see her dress draped over the chair. John must have put her to bed. There was no sign of him. She groaned with shame and pulled her head off the pillow. She rolled off the bed on to her knees and pulled herself up to standing, gulping down the water and heading for the bathroom. The powerful smell of coffee drifted up the stairs. John must still be here. She glimpsed herself in the mirror and put the shower on. He would have to wait until she had made herself look a bit more alive. Her mascara was underneath her tired-looking eyes, and her lips stained with red wine. When she got out of the shower, there was a mug of coffee by the bed with two paracetamols. She marvelled again at how lucky she was to have met John.

Feeling a bit more herself, Marie found John sitting at the kitchen table. He had cleared last night's dishes, and the kitchen was spotless. She sheepishly apologised.

'I wanted our first time to be special,' she said.

'It doesn't matter,' he said, squeezing her hand, 'I'm not going anywhere; we have all the time in the world.' Marie noticed the time; how had she slept so late? It was nearly time to pick up the girls. John offered to get them and take them to the park for waffles whilst she took some time to nurse her hangover.

Marie's hungover mind drifted to thoughts of Carl. She pondered over the short period of time between Carl's death and her spending the night with John. Even though nothing happened, she wanted it to. What kind of wife did that make her? Marie's stomach churned, a mixture of stale alcohol and guilt. Even after his death, Carl still induced anxiety in Marie. She shook her head, taking some deep breaths and eyeing the bathroom door. Thoughts of Carl pushed aside, she just made it to the bathroom in time.

The Professionals

Jenna was back to work on a phased return. She had been off for a while, so lots of her caseload had been reallocated or were no longer on probation. That was going to be one of the hardest things about getting back into the swing of work - getting to know her new caseload. She was told she would be supported and could take things at the pace she needed, but she knew from others that actions and words were not always the same. The trouble was the people on probation had to be seen by someone, so caseloads just kept creeping up. They were all just firefighting. A big part of their jobs was referring offenders for support with housing, counselling, mental health, and other services, but often the wait for these services was so long they ended up giving the interim support themselves. Some workers did the bare minimum, whilst those who went above and beyond would eventually feel it take its toll on their own mental health. Jenna had just about been keeping herself afloat until the relationship break-up and the pregnancy. She was both dreading seeing him and excited to see him in equal measures. After her return-to-work interview and a bit of time looking over her caseload, she popped to the coffee morning at the Social Services building.

'Jenna, great to see you back,' welcomed Beth. 'You're looking so well! I have a couple of families on my caseload that I think are on yours as well, so I'll catch up with you next week when you are settled.'

'Yes, I spotted a few familiar names on my list, so we can chat properly soon. No matter how long you are off, the same old faces are always on the merry-go-round!'

'True, true. Now, who wants a cuppa?' said Emma joining in.

~

'Ugh,' said Katie. 'I have to visit the family of Leanne, the girl who died in the club, to let them know we are no longer actively investigating her death.' There had been no further leads, and her superiors had decided it was not in the public interest to continue their enquiries. She hoped there would have been some sign where the drugs came from on Leanne's phone, but it looked like she had just bought them from a stranger in the club and been unlucky. They got no further information from her friends. Katie felt sure that at least one of them knew something, but no one was talking. Girls that age told each other everything; they must know who she got the drugs from, or at least have seen her talking to someone unfamiliar if they didn't know who it was. Katie called the allocated FLO to see if she was available later, then made the call to Leanne's parents to arrange to visit them later that afternoon. The FLO had supported them since Katie's initial visit, so it was nice that they were both able to attend later.

'Come on then, let's go take your mind off it and get some cake,' said Tom. They logged off the computers they were using and set off for the coffee morning at Social Services.

Bernie

Bernie wanted an easy life. She was not unlike Fiona in many ways, apart from the prostitution. She just wanted to be left alone to feed her small habit and work the streets. Most of her clients these days were regulars, and she knew what she was getting – or it was more a case of they knew what they were getting. She was too old for the constant string of unknown punters and left those for the feisty younger girls. The years had not always been kind to her – one of the risks of the job, and Bernie had the scars to prove it, emotionally and physically.

Bernie didn't know what had come over her trying to skim money off her earnings the other week; it was an uncharacteristic moment of rebellion. Bernie was a woman who could be described as 'salt of the earth'. Nothing was too much trouble for those close to her, and she took on a mother hen figure among the younger street girls. She became a listening ear, a confidante, and encouraged them to keep themselves safe. As safe as they could in this line of work. Bernie was the kind of person who would call you pet, and when that happened, everything felt okay. She had been to Jackie's a couple of times now, and it was clear that Jackie wanted company as much as cleaning. This suited Bernie. She knew there would come a time she couldn't earn her money the way she was, and the cleaning on the side would help.

It was the day for her group, and she was in good spirits. Bernie quite liked the group. She had no intention of changing her drug use; she was happily ticking along as she was. Bernie wasn't court ordered to attend the group, like most of the others, but it was a condition of remaining on her methadone script. She was on a low dose and used a small amount of street heroin on top to hold her habit. The agencies were no longer letting people stay on a script long term without them proving that they were motivated and at least trying to stop the drugs and change their ways. Bernie had a good relationship with her Drug Worker, Kylie, and the group wasn't too demanding. Bernie enjoyed the company. As she approached the building, Frank was outside smoking. He asked her for a lighter, and she gave him one, lighting herself a cigarette afterwards.

'How are you holding up, pet?' He had had a few drinks, and his ruddy complexion was emphasized by the slightly glazed look in his eyes.

'I miss her so much. Why does everything go wrong?' He was clearly in self-pity mode. She felt for him, but this man never seemed to help himself. One of life's self-appointed victims. 'I am just so lonely,' he said.

She moved closer and rubbed his forearm, making soothing sounds. He suddenly lurched towards her, head tilted, eyes closed, stumbling slightly as she took a shocked step sideways. She might be getting on, but street workers were always quick on their feet, a necessary skill she had to develop. Bernie tactfully rebuffed Frank's advances. She gently reminded him he was hurting right now, and it was too soon to be moving on.

'See, nothing goes right. Even someone who fucks for a living won't shag me.'

Bernie bristled. Frank had crossed the line. She hated when men assumed that because she took money for sex, it took away her right to decide who she had sex with.

'I'm going on in.' Her tone was clipped as she stubbed her cigarette out. She put the chipped end carefully back in the packet for later and strode past Frank into Phoenix.

Her

It worked out so wonderfully; she couldn't have planned it better if she had tried. She happened to be at the MacMillan morning when a couple of the workers from the rough sleeper team had dropped in. They had asked her if she would bring any leftover cakes away at the end of the day to hand out early the next morning on their rounds. It was an early start, and she was up at 5 am, ready to meet the team in town. She had added her Lily of the Valley flapjacks to the bag of snacks and was on her way. The team had a list of specific people and places to visit. For someone to be deemed homeless and therefore eligible for emergency accommodation through the council, they had to be seen rough sleeping. This meant that people who had a friend to stay with slipped through the net somewhat as you were not considered urgent until you were sleeping on the street.

It was the same old issue that she had been seeing since she was younger. Often those beyond help were the ones that got offered the most. By the time they failed to turn up for appointments and got kicked to the bottom of the waiting lists, the next person who may have just needed a bit of a helping hand had now hit rock bottom, and the cycle started all over again. There must be a way to save these people from hitting that rock bottom. To save them from reaching desperation –

the depths of despair that her mother ended up in. No child should have to be the one playing the parent. She saw it all too often, and counted her blessings every day that she hadn't gone down the route that many did – ending up in the care system, often in a cycle of abuse, turning to drugs and drink to get through the day. She understood, she really did. But empathy for their situation doesn't change anything. If they aren't willing to help themselves, she needed to get out there and try to save the people that were still worth helping.

The rough sleeper team visited various spots where specific people spent the night – usually doorways or steps up to buildings. It was hard because if you had anything worth stealing, such as drugs or drink, you were left vulnerable on your own. If you did group with others, the only choice you had was to trust them… to a certain extent. They visited one older man who told her he had been in the military but ended up homeless, following mental health issues. He didn't want accommodation and said he was happier on the street as it was all he knew now. The team visited him and gave him clean clothes, food and drink and someone to talk to if he wanted it. They checked in with a couple sleeping under a bridge in a tiny tent. She already knew the couple as she had worked with both of them over the years. The girl was offered accommodation but refused to take it unless her boyfriend was allowed to go with her - she'd rather stay with him than take a bed in a safe place, so they remained on the streets. These women made her blood boil – turning down help for a lowlife who knocks her about. This was a classic example of how much time and energy was wasted on certain individuals. The couple were both on probation and were well known to police for petty offences. They had more than one baby removed at birth and placed in adoption and often had the police and/ or ambulance service called when they fought. Her boyfriend had served more than one jail sentence for his abuse of her, and previous partners, but each time he was released, back she went. She tried to help, she offered a supportive ear, but eventually, it came back to the old moral query; if these two weren't constantly wasting blue light resources, could more people be saved? Should these two be sacrificed for the sake of many others? The guy was a scumbag anyway, and she was, quite frankly, pathetic. She kept her thoughts to herself.

After handing over supplies and advice that fell on deaf ears, they headed for the car park. The biggest group of people would be here, and this was the last place on the list to visit. When they got there, she had the flapjacks ready. Her heart raced as her hands closed around them in her coat pockets. She helpfully unwrapped them as she handed them out, thinking this would encourage the homeless to eat them straight away. It also meant she could take any potentially incriminating wrapping away with her. Her eyes glinted in the moonlight, the excitement on her face masked only by the shadows as she watched some of them take their first bite. It was like a second self-took over and her senses heightened, the buzz pulsing through her veins at the mission, and the consequences should be caught. They didn't stay long, just long enough to hand out supplies and make a note of who was sleeping there. Daylight was almost upon them, and it was time to go home and change, ready for the day job. She thanked the team for taking her out with them, slipping the remaining few flapjacks into her pocket for disposal.

The Professionals

The call came from a member of staff at one of the local hostels who had gone out looking for a client who failed to attend an appointment. The client was a regular at the car park, and she had gone there looking for her. She immediately called 999 and sent a text to Tom. She still had his number from the brief fling they'd had a while ago. She suspected his wife found out, when it came to an abrupt ending. There were no hard feelings on her part. She knew he was married, and it was only a bit of fun. They were useful contacts for each other now, when it came to information sharing.

It wasn't long before three police cars arrived, along with two ambulances. She'd already put two people into recovery positions and was relieved when the professionals took over. The environment was not safe - with broken glass and a risk of needle stick injuries. Aside from the risk of being jabbed with a needle, she knew some rough sleepers carried knives or other weapons for protection, so was wary of providing first aid. Tom arrived not long after the cavalry, and she debriefed him before returning to the hostel.

Word was soon circulated following the incident. One person was pronounced dead at the scene, two had been taken to hospital unresponsive, and a further four had been taken for monitoring following sickness and dizziness. The hospital hadn't yet identified the cause of the incident. Tom spoke with the rough sleeper team, who assured him there were no issues when they attended in the early hours. They had handed out food all over the city that morning, so he discounted food poisoning as only the car park assembly had become ill. He couldn't shake the feeling that he was missing something. They would need to investigate drugs, or perhaps there was some dodgy home brew going around that had caused issues before. Every now and then, they would find someone had a go at making their own hooch. It never ended well as the stuff was strong and potentially lethal.

~

Jenna escaped seeing Tom until she popped into Phoenix for a three-way with Kylie and one of their mutual clients. She wasn't expecting to see him, and her heart began to race. She was dizzy, her breath caught in her throat. Her face flushed as he passed her in the corridor and said 'alright' with that familiar cheeky smile before pushing through the double doors and disappearing down the stairs. She tried to regain her composure and told Kylie she would catch her up, running into a vacant interview room and sinking down against the wall. When she felt overwhelmed or anxious, she took deep breaths and used the techniques her counsellor told her to use. She looked around, telling herself she was safe and focusing on what she could see in the room. The room was sparse, but she looked at the items of furniture in turn, and gripped the cool metal leg of the chair next to her until she felt her anxiety begin to subside. She took out her phone and messaged Anna and Grace, *Have just seen him. He was completely normal, WTF,*

159

debrief needed when I'm back'. She went back out into the foyer and found Kylie making small talk with her client whilst they waited for her to join them.

Jenna had a busy day. It was all very well having a phased return, but it felt like that meant she had the same amount of people on her caseload, but with fewer days to manage it. Following the meeting at Phoenix, she made her way back to the probation office and felt a lot more at ease by the time she got there. Her heart rate had returned to normal and her hands no longer shook. Grace and Anna were waiting, prepared to rally around her, but she found she was okay. She had an appointment with her high-profile case that afternoon – the recently released Head Teacher, convicted of historic sex offences. She had his case on her caseload while he was still in custody, so she had good background knowledge. Though, whilst he was in custody, she had had little to do with him, except for the couple of times he had attempted to get an early release. He was going to need a full Offender Assessment interview where she would have to make a judgement on his risk of re-offending. The buck stopped with her, and if she didn't get this right, she would be the one who would come under fire if he re-offended. It was maddening that when they repeat offended, screwing up again and again, the public blamed the probation officer just as much as the offender. It was as if they thought she had a crystal ball to see into and determine if someone might do something bad. Generally, the public view was that offenders, especially sex offenders, should be locked up and have the key thrown away - Jenna believed that he deserved a chance to change just as much as anyone else. She was passionate about giving people opportunities and making sure that society's judgement didn't hold them back. She heard the tannoy announcing her appointment was waiting in reception and made her way down with a sigh.

Jenna's parents couldn't understand how she could work with paedophiles. Her dad always said he was worried for her safety – she reassured them she was about 20 years too old for most of them, so Arthur was probably one of the safest and most predictable of her caseload to be in a room with. After the appointment, Jenna emailed Beth to arrange an appointment to discuss the assessment once it had been written up. Arthur said he wanted contact with his grandchildren, so this would need to be carefully considered and managed between them. The media would love to get hold of a story about how probation let a convicted paedophile be around children, and if anything were to happen… even doing everything by the book, the press would be quick to vilify Jenna.

~

Katie attended Leanne's funeral, sitting at the back in full dress uniform. Her body felt overwhelmed with sadness at the injustice of someone so young being taken. She thought she should find it easier in her job as time went on, but it didn't get any easier. Her struggles reminded her of her humanity. Some colleagues were completely desensitised and seemed unaffected – she saw the looks they gave her when she struggled to conceal her emotions. This was a hard industry to work in. Katie saw the gentlest of souls become broken shells, their heart locked away, protecting them from the horrors their job often exposed them to. In turn, keeping their heart locked away from their own life. The force was getting better, but it was still a man's world. The old gentleman's club opening mocking the weak – those brave enough to ask for counselling or support. Their requests, not only met with institutional mockery, but often budgetary restraints, meaning they had to just get on with it. Katie was proud to be a police officer, proud to serve her country but couldn't wait for the day when the rigid criminal justice services caught up with the therapeutic interventions they operated alongside.

These poor parents shouldn't have to bury their child. She was filled with admiration for the celebrant and how she kept her composure during what was an emotional service. Katie paid her respects to the family as she left to return to the station. Tom was waiting for her when she got back, ready to put the kettle on and provide a listening ear if she needed it. For all his faults when it came to women and relationships, she could always rely on Tom to know when she needed him. That was the good side of policing – you had to have each other's backs. You went into potentially volatile situations, and if you didn't support each other, there was a risk you would both get killed. Not all colleagues extended this support outside of life-or-death scenarios, but Katie was lucky to be in the same team as Tom, who had a more modern approach.

'It just feels like one death after another lately,' he mused. 'If I didn't know better, I would think there was someone out there, bumping off the scrotes of Plymouth.'

'Leanne was *not* a scrote; she was an innocent schoolgirl,' defended Katie.

'Whatever, there still seem to have been too many deaths lately.'

Tilly

Tilly wanted to attend the funeral with Luke, but her mother insisted they go as a family. Her mother was being over the top as usual with a black fascinator and full-on dramatic hair and makeup. Tilly couldn't help but think what a wonderful grieving widow her mother would make if anything ever happened to her father. Efford Crematorium had expansive grounds that were beautifully cared for. The paths were lined with cherry blossom trees, and lovely old stone walls surrounded the gardens. If you didn't notice the graves, you might think you were in the grounds of a National Trust property. It was busy, and crowds were gathering, waiting for the earlier funeral to finish and filter out of the back door, ready for Leanne's mourners to take their places. Leanne's class had been given the day off school if they wanted, and there were many of her classmates amongst those standing in the sunshine. Tilly spotted their Head Teacher, along with a couple of other teachers and staff from the school. Sudden silence shifted the atmosphere, and people parted as the hearse carrying the coffin drove through the crowds. Leanne's family were in cars behind. Her parents and younger brother got out with what Tilly assumed to be her grandparents. They all stood by the door to the crematorium while the coffin was brought out and pall bearers took their positions. Leanne's younger brother was fidgeting with his tie. Tilly wanted to run. The guilt was all-consuming, and she wanted to turn and run as fast and as far away as her legs would take her. She wanted her friend back. She wished she could turn the clock back and that they hadn't gone out that night. She heard a loud sob escape from her mouth, and her mother put an arm around her. It gave her little comfort. She made it through the service, her heart aching as she watched the slideshow. Images of them at school, at birthday parties growing up, and on various nights out flashed across the screen. She wanted to block out the pain and make these feelings go away. At the wake, she took a bottle of wine from the table, unnoticed and sat outside on a bench drinking it until Luke came and wrapped his arms around her. His big arms made her feel safe, as if nothing in the world could get to her. He took her back to his flat and sat with her while she cried. She wanted to tell him; she had to tell someone, but all that came out was more sobs that Luke shhhed as he held her.

Bernie

No-one answered the door when Bernie arrived at Jackie's, and Bernie was not sure what to do. What if Jackie had fallen? But then she didn't know if she should just go in. She decided to try the door, and if it was locked, that would decide for her. As she turned the handle and pushed it open, she shouted hello with no response. She put her bag down in the hallway and shouted hello again at the bottom of the stairs. There was no sign of anyone in the downstairs rooms, so she tentatively made her way up the stairs. The curtains were still drawn on the landing, highlighting the artificial light from the computer coming under the door from James' room. Bernie stepped towards his door, feeling nervous. There was something about that boy that put her on edge. As she put her hand out to push the door open, it opened in front of her, and James appeared.

'Can I help you?'

'Just looking for your mum.'

'She's out. You know my room is private.' he said. Bernie felt uncomfortable, the unspoken warning hanging in the air. She stepped back while he locked the door as they stood together on the landing. 'Just carry on with whatever you need to do. I'm sure Mum will be back soon.' Just then, they heard the door downstairs, and Jackie shouted up the stairs that she was sorry she was late and would get the kettle on. Bernie breathed a sigh of relief and scurried away from James as quickly as she could without letting him know she was unnerved. If there was one thing she knew about men, it was to never let them see fear or weakness. She couldn't help but wonder what was in his room that he was so secretive about. Jackie spoke about James very little. She said he was going to achieve big things one day, and seemed to think his love of computers meant he would be the next Steve Jobs. She told Bernie about Luke's girlfriend and how she looked forward to meeting the girl. She sounded so proud when she spoke about Luke. She described him as a local businessman – anyone who heard Jackie speak of him would have no idea he made his living selling drugs and women. Bernie sometimes wondered if Jackie had actually convinced herself he was a legitimate businessman by the way she spoke.

Bernie and Luke had their ups and downs, but she knew she had crossed the line when he set his heavies on her. Now knowing where he came from, Bernie saw the little boy who grew up doing all he could to provide for his mum and little brother. It was sad, but realistically, when someone had a shitty upbringing like his, there was a good chance you would end up on the wrong path. Luke and Bernie both ended up on that same path, just on different sides of the fence. She didn't condone what he had done to her, but she knew the rules of the street were there for a reason. She didn't even know why she had lied about her takings; it was a silly moment of rebellion. Even as a child, Bernie always saw the good in others and never could hold a grudge.

Her

She hadn't known what to expect from the flapjack/ lily of the valley plan after carrying it out. One thing she hadn't expected was the reaction from the local news and the community. The story had made the front page of the Plymouth Herald, with reporters sharing how many ambulances, police cars and public resources had been required to attend. Whilst, technically on this occasion, it was her fault, it was for a greater good. The local community appeared to share her views on the victims, and the comments on the Facebook article were filled with vitriol for the addicts and street drinkers affected. One person dead, and a further two were still in hospital. She hoped that if they survived, they might take the time to evaluate their lives. The near-death experience might be the catalyst for realising something had to change. She doubted it, but she tried to hold on to that last bit of belief she had buried inside her. A few of the others had been treated at the hospital for sickness, confusion, and some unpleasant sounding gastro-related issues. An email was circulated around local agencies detailing the incident. Whilst the cause was still unknown, the email advised that further investigation was underway and malicious actions hadn't been ruled out. She heard that some of the rough sleeper team had been questioned over it – being asked if they had seen anything suspicious and what state the group was in when they visited. She would need to step back a bit and be careful whilst the dust settled after this latest victory. She smiled again, looking over the online article and the ever-increasing comments.

As she scrolled, another article caught her eye. She knew the face of the evil Head Teacher; everyone locally would know that face, even if they weren't around when he committed his crimes. He was a regular feature in local press – appearing each time he applied for parole, or when his victims were in the news. A sordid reminder of why they ended up the way they did. Occasionally there would be an article about Plymouth's worst predators – his was always the first stock photo to be added to the pile of those with his predilections. She knew he had been released recently but hadn't given him much thought. Until now. She would monitor his case and see if he had learned from his past. Would he be the one who surprised her? Because good guys were thin on the ground right now, and she was beginning to think that rehabilitation was a lost cause. Yes, he might be a worthwhile project in the future if he failed to prove himself. She wanted to believe that he would have been released and rehabilitated, but experience taught her that leopards rarely changed their spots. Once upon a time, she was fresh faced and full of plans to change the world. These days, she knew it was more about making appropriate sacrifices for the greater good.

She had always prided herself on her independence and fierce loyalty to friends, but she found herself thinking, not for the first time, how she wished she had someone to confide in about all this. Yes, she had stopped dating because it was so tedious and time consuming, but on the flip side, to meet someone like minded would be special. She took a deep breath in, nosily exhaling and puffing out her cheeks. What was she thinking? Even if she did meet someone, she couldn't very well ask if she could run the pros and cons of her latest plan by them. Her mother trusted someone and let him into her life, and she never recovered. He didn't care about the destruction he walked away from, and society didn't care enough to prioritise her. No, she was better off alone.

Frank

Frank was drunk again. He couldn't believe what happened with Bernie, not only that he made a pass at her, but what he said afterwards. Every time he thought of it, he felt shame wash over his body. He kept trying to catch her eye during the group, but she wouldn't look at him. She hadn't made him a cup of tea during the break like she usually did, and she wasn't outside smoking before the group or during the break. He liked Bernie and was annoyed that he had offended her. In his drunken state, it seemed like it would be a good idea to make his way towards Docker Street, where the street workers were. Frank was not a bad man, he didn't have bad intentions, he just didn't seem to get things right. If he could find her, he could apologise and make it better. She would pat him on the shoulder, forgive him, and call him pet again. Only, it didn't go to plan. When Frank got there, he couldn't find Bernie. He asked around and, typical; she wasn't working that night. He was offered solace by one of the other girls, and he mistook this for a chance to gain the comfort he so craved. The alcohol no longer provided the warm comfort blanket it used to, and Frank sought human touch.

Afterwards, he felt dirty. What happened in the back alley was not a connection, and it was not comfort. She was mechanical, impersonal and had a vacant look in her eyes. He hadn't noticed how spaced out she was until he tried to make eye contact when they were having sex. He had to get home. Frank pushed her away, paid her and started walking home. He took the familiar route along The Hoe and Barbican. The seafront was always busy in the early evening - runners out exercising, couples walking with ice creams for romantic outings, families that had been out enjoying the fresh air and open space savouring the last hours of daylight.

The next morning, Frank woke up with the all too familiar feeling of regret. This was his life. Every day, his first thought was shame. Shame that washed over his body, closely followed by the regret that made him squeeze his eyes shut and turn over, pulling the duvet over his head. His mum woke him again with annoyance. Apparently, he had left the front door open when he came home and smashed her favourite vase as he stumbled to his room. She stood in his bedroom doorway, her face a mask of disappointment. Her sad eyes were downcast as she turned away, pulling the door closed. Frank's heart broke at the stifled sob from the hallway before the footsteps retreated downstairs. He sometimes felt as if she would be better off without him. At least she could get on with her life without him constantly disappointing her. Perhaps then she would be able to rebuild her friendships and volunteer for the church again without being told they already had enough volunteers for any event she put herself forward for. She would get her life back.

Her

She was out running. She took her regular route along The Hoe, following the water's edge around to the cobbled streets of The Barbican. She liked the anonymity of running. No-one ever noticed her, dressed in black, silently pounding the pavements, blending in. People might remember seeing someone, maybe a runner, but they would remember no specifics. She saw the same faces, the same people who went for a walk after work, children from the local flats playing in the park at West Hoe. She saw the surreptitious drug deals and the same groups of teenagers hanging around. She often saw Frank along her route, as he often drank at the pubs along The Hoe and Barbican. She mulled over his fate. He had sealed it himself, really. It didn't matter if she intervened or if she left it to him; he was destroying his life and slowly killing himself. The question was, how long could she stand by watching and waiting for him to hurt more people along the way? She knew she had to wait for the right moment and think her plan through carefully. He told the group last week that he was feeling low. She knew he was having some suicidal thoughts and was mulling over a plan where she could exploit those. Perhaps, with some carefully planned encouragement, he could be persuaded to do the job himself. She would have to give it some more thought.

If Frank stopped drinking and proved he had changed, she wouldn't need to get rid of him. He had to make his choices, and the consequences were down to him. If he had to be sacrificed to give his mum a chance to have a life again, and to take away the risk of him hurting someone else through his actions when drunk again, then so be it.

If Dylan's mum hadn't drunk the poisoned vodka, putting her needs before those of her son, she would still be alive. If those pathetic wasters on the street had got their acts together, they wouldn't have been scrounging food and wouldn't have had the flapjacks. All of their fates could have been avoided if they had taken the right path. Everyone was in control of their future; they had a choice, and she only stepped in if they made the wrong one. She was sure most of their family members would thank her if they could. Society certainly would. She wouldn't use the word saviour exactly, but her heart swelled with pride when she thought about how she was helping others to have the chances that no one gave her mother.

The Plymouth Herald was still reporting the 'dark side of the streets of Plymouth'. They continued to report on the incident in the car park with pleas for Plymouth's leaders to take action to tackle the crime, homelessness and addiction that the streets were plagued with. It was good for her that police resources were too stretched to do too much investigating, and it was currently believed that a bad batch of drugs had circulated. Even though a couple of those affected were drinkers, it was just suspected that they were also dabbling in drugs that night.

The Professionals

Tom was at the station preparing for the last addiction group when he heard the call over the radio for a unit to attend the school opposite Phoenix. He answered and said he was heading that way, anyway. There were reports of a suspicious male loitering outside. When he got there, there was no one around, but he paid a quick visit to the Head Teacher to reassure her that he had attended and had a look around. He advised her he was over the road for the next few hours and told her to give Phoenix a call and ask for him if there were any further concerns.

Tom headed back to Phoenix to prepare for the group with Sally, noticing an email from Beth that he had been copied into. She was meeting with Jenna about the noncing Head Teacher and was checking if he wanted to attend as he was the one who raised concerns about the grandchildren. Jenna seemed to be less of a mental case these days, and he had heard nothing on the rumour mill to the contrary, so he hoped it would be safe to attend. Why were some women such a pain? Why couldn't they accept a fling for what it was? They were so needy.

Tom was usually upfront about being married, or said he wasn't looking for a relationship, but women always thought they could change him. He loved his wife, and his heart dropped to his stomach the time she threatened to leave him. He couldn't imagine his life without her, and he tried so hard to live his life with only her. He just also loved the adrenaline buzz and excitement that came with meeting someone new. The thrill of chase, the feeling of being wanted, and unpredictable sex.

~

The last group went well, and Grace, Kylie, Sally, Emma, Tom, and Anna were all in attendance for the end of the session to meet with the participants individually and discuss future goals and plans. Each participant would receive a report that would be shared with whichever agency had referred them. Sally spoke about the importance of building healthy relationships and promoted Revive. Kylie gave information on ongoing support groups around addiction, and Anna spoke for probation, advising that those on probation would be sent a follow-up appointment to review progress and discuss any further requirements on their licences or Community Orders. Emma thanked everyone for their progress and attendance and, just like that, another group was finished.

Frank had been pissed as usual, and they would all be glad to see the back of his increasingly belligerent and self-pitying behaviour. They would spend the next few weeks finishing up the paperwork and preparing for the next group. The facilitators for each course varied, and whoever was on the next one would be meeting with the next lot of participants. The multi-agency approach to the groups was relatively new, but it seemed to tick the boxes. Whether it was doing any good was yet to be seen.

~

Beth and Emma headed to Costa before work for a natter and a catch up.

'It feels like ages since you have come over to ours,' Beth said, 'why don't you bring Ryan, and we will have a barbecue at the weekend? Stay over so you can have a few drinks. The kids will love a sleepover.'

'Sounds good,' Emma smiled. They headed back to the office, ready to face the day. Beth was off to meet with Jenna at probation. She arrived at the same time Tom pulled into the car park, and they headed in together. Arthur McIntyre was in reception early when they passed through. They nodded in acknowledgement and went in search of Jenna. Beth had already spoken with Arthur's daughter, who said she had no intention of stopping her dad from seeing his grandchildren. She said they were already close to their grandmother and were gradually getting used to their grandad being on the scene. He had been in prison when they were born, so it was going to take some time to build that relationship and for them to get used to sharing their granny. His daughter maintained Arthur's innocence, however, said that the children would not be left alone with him because of his age and them not having had much of a relationship with him.

'My concern,' mused Beth, 'is that she is still not acknowledging the potential risk. She says that he won't be left alone with the children, but this is not because she is consciously safeguarding them. It is for other reasons.' Beth went on to say that she suspected the daughter's unwavering belief that her dad was innocent was starting to crack now she was faced with the reality of her own children starting to form a relationship with him.

'What does her husband make of it all?' asked Tom.

'That's the thing, he works away a lot and is happy to trust her judgement. He isn't from around here, and I don't know if he fully understands quite how prolific this case was and how it impacted, and still impacts, our community.' Jenna said she was happy to be led by Beth on this one. The matter had been discussed prior to his release, but at that time, his licence terms had simply been that he was not to have unsupervised contact with anyone under 18. This was agreed upon his release. After a lengthy discussion, the consensus was to add the addendum to his licence agreement, that he could have contact with his grandchildren, but this must be supervised by his daughter or son-in-law. If the children were to spend time alone with their grandmother, he would either need to leave the property for the duration of the visit, or it would need to be conducted elsewhere.

'Right, I'll let him know,' said Jenna.

'Do you want me to come?' Tom offered.

'Oh, now you care? Bit bloody late,' snapped Jenna, nodding goodbye to Beth and heading down to reception. Beth raised an eyebrow and smirked. She couldn't wait to pick that little interaction apart with Emma.

~

Jenna's pulse sped, heat flushing through her body as she clenched her teeth together. How could Tom attend a meeting like that as if nothing happened? She felt like she was going mad and had imagined the whole affair. As she left, she chided herself for the bitchy comment. Why couldn't she hold it in?

And who did he think he was offering to swoop in and protect her now?

Arthur was still in reception, waiting patiently. He was always early. She grabbed a personal alarm from reception as a precaution and led him through to an interview room. He accepted the news. If he was unhappy, he didn't show it beyond asking if this could be reviewed at some point. Jenna agreed she was happy to review this in six months when he was more settled and had completed some offending behaviour work. Jenna kept the meeting short and factual for today, giving Arthur his appointment slip for the following week and instructions to let her know if he needed anything. Arthur shook her hand, thanking her for her support and made his way out. Jenna was already half way up the stairs before he made it to the door. *Fucking Tom,* she thought as she left the interview room, stomping upstairs towards the safety of her desk, their meeting spinning in her mind. She probably should have spent a bit more time with Arthur, but thoughts of Tom managed to occupy all the space in her head.

Luke

'I want you to meet my mum,' Luke said to Tilly lying beside to her. 'I know she'll love you as much as I do.'

'You love me?' asked Tilly.

'That's right, Tilly Josephine Anderson, I love you,' declared Luke, kissing her lightly on the tip of her nose.

'I love you too,' she whispered, her eyes glistening as she turned away. Luke jumped out of bed and kissed her again before turning on the shower in the en-suite. He didn't hear her add quietly, 'You wouldn't love me if you knew what I have done.'

It was Tilly's birthday the following week; she would finally be 18, and he was looking forward to taking her away the weekend after. Her mum seemed to finally be accepting that she couldn't keep trying to control Tilly, and he could see her more often. Luke was planning to wine and dine Tilly with a weekend in Cardiff. He showered and left Tilly in bed while he went out to check on some business and pick up food for them.

Business was going well, and Luke had a good group of lads that he trusted working for him. He knew that he had done well in this game to swerve a prison sentence so far, and he was planning to invest in some more legitimate businesses now he had the capital. He already had a tattoo parlour that he was laundering money through, and he was building a nest egg to make some proper investments. In the future, he could see them running a property empire. Luke knew Tilly wasn't stupid and had sussed out some of his business dealings, but he hadn't filled in the gaps. He knew he would need to be more honest with her and see how she took it. This was not the 1950s, when the women had to stay at home without knowing the details of their husband's business dealings. If he and Tilly were going to be together, he wanted to be honest with her. He got the impression she would enjoy being hands-on. Perhaps he would have a chat with her and see if she fancied her own little business. He could buy something for her to run, and he could run money through her books when he needed to. It would keep Tilly occupied without getting her into anything illegal.

Luke tried to get his brother involved to give him some purpose and a chance to earn some money, but James had turned him down. Their mum would throttle Luke if she found out, but Luke just wanted to encourage James to get out and about and be a bit more normal. It isn't healthy being shut away in the bedroom, glued to a computer. Luke didn't hold back on his thoughts that James should be out meeting people and living his life. It sometimes occurred to him that his mum might like that James didn't have much of a life, as it meant she got to keep her baby at home with her.

Marie

Since the shame of the night when she had invited John over for sex and proceeded to get too drunk to follow it through, Marie hadn't had another opportunity. They had been busy with the girls, and it seemed every other day there was another classmate's birthday party or play date to attend. The girls loved having John around and seemed to flourish with his attention. Alice once asked if John was their daddy now. John had said that Daddy Carl would always be their Daddy, but that if they and their mummy would like, he hoped to be around and do lots of the things daddy Carl couldn't do with them anymore. Marie's heart felt like it would burst out of her chest as she heard this exchange, and she nodded at him as her eyes filled with tears of happiness. She could never say that Carl didn't love his girls, but he wasn't there for them like he should have been. This quality time that John spent with them is something they should have had with Carl, but he was more interested in being at the pub with his mates, where he could tell everyone what a wonderful dad he was. Marie felt a pang of sadness when she thought back over their life, trying to figure out when it all went wrong. She shouldn't have allowed him to continue putting his hands on her, but she didn't know how to make him stop. She initially hoped it was just a phase, but then it became habit, and it was too late to do anything about it. She got used to covering the bruises, and judging his mood so she could try not to antagonise him. Marie thought no-one noticed, that it was easy to cover up his behaviour because he had already alienated most of her friends. She didn't see many people, and the ones she did, didn't ask. At least he never laid a finger on the girls. Even though he wasn't really there for them, they loved him and would never have hurt them.

'So, you haven't shagged him yet?' Marie's friend asked. She was enjoying a catch-up with Mandy while John looked after the girls. Marie was trying to rebuild some of the friendships lost during her marriage to Carl. Some of her friends didn't want to know, but luckily Mandy was not one of them. Mandy was struggling to understand how Marie and John had got to this point without sex. Marie tried to explain their closeness and how sex hadn't seemed to matter; their relationship was more than that. As she said it out loud, she heard how shallow it sounded, but continued, saying he wasn't pushing for it and was patient and understanding.

'Anyway, it's still early days. Carl only just died!'

'But don't YOU want it?' said Mandy. 'Is he gay?' she continued without waiting for an answer.

Marie did want it. She kept making excuses and saying how kind and loving John was, but the truth was, she was impatient. She sometimes felt like he was avoiding situations where it might happen, making sure they were not alone, or he would say he thought he heard one of the girls awake or he had to be up early. Often, he would go home after the girls were in bed, saying he slept better in his own bed. Marie couldn't say it out loud as she felt like a horrible person, but she sometimes felt he was only with her for the girls – it was as if he just wanted a readymade family. He was such a good father figure to them, and she sometimes felt second best. Those poor girls had just lost their dad, and here she was, jealous that John gave them more attention than her. She changed the subject with Mandy, asking for updates on what their old gang of friends had been up to in the past few years.

The Professionals

Beth needed to arrange a check-in with Dylan and his grandparents. His grandmother answered the phone and said her husband was at the golf course catching up with an old friend. Beth wasn't working this weekend, so they arranged the visit for the following week. Beth sent a quick email to the school requesting an update on Dylan's progress and engagement. Just as she was about to log off, she saw an email asking if she fancied a drink after work; it looked like some of the probation girls were heading to Wetherspoons to properly welcome Jenna back to work. Curiosity got the better of her, remembering that frosty exchange between Jenna and Tom, and she replied, saying she would meet them there. It would have to be a quick one as she had been working late more and more often lately, and she needed to make sure she was putting the hours in at home with her family. It was so hard as a social worker. You ended up spending so much time checking on other people's families and making sure they were okay and had the right support, that it was easy to neglect your own family or miss things. The caseloads and stress were at an all-time high, and those who stuck it out often did so at the detriment of their own relationships.

~

Katie didn't know what to make of the latest case she had been asked to look into. There had been a report of a safeguarding concern put into Social Services about a family she had worked with a fair bit. The husband had been abusive and died a couple of months back in an accident on The Barbican. The wife seemed to be in a new relationship already, because why wait to grieve and deal with your emotions properly? The report referenced concerns about the new boyfriend. Katie had spoken with the duty social worker, who had triaged it as not being a high priority but that it warranted some investigation. It seemed someone he had previously dated had reported that she had concerns about him being around children. Given the nature of the complaint, the lack of evidence and no reason to suspect imminent risk, they agreed to wait until next week before visiting. It was a delicate subject, and they agreed Katie would speak to him at work and follow up with his ex, whilst the duty worker would try to arrange for Marie's previous social worker, Beth, to visit her. Often these sorts of reports from ex-partners turned out to be malicious.

Her

It was late, and the streetlights were casting shadows in the moonlight. The route from The Hoe to The Barbican always had a unique feel at night. You could feel completely alone, yet hear the odd shout or sounds echoing off the water. There were old walls and sea caves along the route, benches in alcoves and closed ice cream and drinks kiosks. She kept running this exact route waiting for her moment. She often saw Frank, but there would be a dog walker or a couple, the headlights of a car illuminating them as it passed by. The opportunity was never quite right, so she would pull her cap down low and continue past him. He never recognised her, never stopped to look, too busy trying to put one foot in front of the other. Tonight felt different. The anticipation and adrenaline ran through her as she set off on her usual run. Her stomach was filled with butterflies; she felt a bit sick. She wasn't sure how it would happen, but she ran over her options again. Last week she had thought she might convince him to jump and use his low mood and suicidal thoughts to save her the job. Or perhaps she would catch him drunk enough to just push him? The pavement was high above the sea, jagged rocks below and a strong current. There was a waist-height wall stopping pedestrians from being able to step off the edge. In some parts, this was reduced to rails, but either way, it would be hard to push anyone over the edge, let alone someone of his stature. Even if he had enough to drink that he didn't resist, or she hit him first, it would take some effort and increase the chances of her being seen. She thought about blowing her cover to lure him down the steps to sit on the rocks under the guise of being a listening ear. It would be easier to push him, but less of a fall. She knew this was a risky plan, but she was new to this. She needed to refine her methods and find more reliable strategies. Her professional experience, together with her natural cynicism, told her that death was the only way out of his pathetic-looking future.

However it happened; something told her tonight was the night. Everything had worked out so far, even when she didn't have all the details figured out. It was as if there was someone looking out for her, recognising that her actions were for a greater good.

The Professionals

Katie pulled up outside a nice-looking property in Ivybridge, on the outskirts of Plymouth. She was there to visit John's ex, who had raised the safeguarding concern. She knew she was stereotyping, but she expected the place to be shabbier. The small front garden was neat and tidy, with smart, colourful hanging baskets by the front door. The girl who answered the door was nothing like Marie. John doesn't have a set type, observed Katie. Steph was younger and much fresher-faced without that jaded look Marie wore. She was dressed in jeans and a camisole, with her dark hair pulled into a short ponytail. She answered the door with a smile ushering Katie through to a kitchen diner. The fridge was covered with children's artwork, and framed school photos smiled down at her from the wall. Katie declined a cup of tea and eased into the conversation with some polite comments about the artwork on the fridge, asking how old the children were before bringing the conversation around to John.

'As I mentioned on the phone, we were informed of your report to the Safeguarding Board and wanted to chat with you about your relationship with John,' she started, 'What can you tell me?' Katie learned that the relationship had been short, less than six months. They met in the park where Katie had been with her children. She said he just came over and asked her out. She had been impressed with his confidence and pleased to meet someone after being single for a while.

'It's hard to find time to date or meet new people as a single mum,' Steph said. The relationship moved quickly, and John seemed too good to be true. She said he was slow to move their relationship forward physically, again, something she appreciated after being single for a while, but was always thoughtful with little gifts for her and the children. He often surprised them with tickets to Zoos or Theme Parks, or offered to look after the kids while Steph met friends or had a pamper day.

'What changed?' Katie probed.

'I don't know. There wasn't anything in particular. I just saw a look in his eyes that made me uncomfortable when he didn't realise I was watching him. At first, I felt like he went out of his way to show me the kids were not a problem, but it soon felt like he was more interested in spending time with them than me. We weren't together long enough for me to leave him alone with them much, but he often offered. We didn't spend much time together one to one. He was always secretive about his phone. I thought maybe he was married, but he wouldn't have been able to spend as much time with us as he did if he was.'

'How did the relationship end?'

'I ended it. He didn't take it well at first and sent loads of begging messages saying he was missing me and the kids. Said I wasn't being fair letting him build a relationship with them and then taking that away. He turned up at the kid's school a couple of times, trying to speak to them at playtime. He was asked to leave, and they threatened him with calling the police. He didn't show up again after that. That was last year, and I

189

haven't seen or heard anything of him since. We moved house, so he doesn't know where we live anymore, anyway.' Katie gleaned Steph had seen him in Central Park when she was visiting friends in Plymouth and recognised the same look when he was looking at the children of the woman he was with. She couldn't put her finger on it, but something compelled her to report it.

'He just gives me the heebie-jeebies. Something isn't right, and I just don't know what.'

Katie thanked Steph for her time and left. There was no need for a follow-up, but Katie planned to pay a visit to John anyway. It was difficult when there was no evidence or anything tangible to back up a feeling, but Katie knew that often those gut feelings were not without reason. In her opinion, Steph presented as credible, and this was one of those occasions where her professional head said to leave it alone as there was no evidence, but her heart said there was something more to this. She headed back to the office, stopping to pick up some doughnuts for her colleagues on the way. It may be cliché, but her colleagues at the station sure did love a doughnut!

~

'For fuck's sake,' said Tom, as he got off the phone, 'what is going on out there?'

Katie looked at him inquisitively.

'Just been informed by uniform that they have found the body of one of the chaps from the addiction course we just finished. Bit of a buffoon, but not a nasty man. He certainly didn't deserve death. Frank, you know the drink driver who killed those young girls that I arrested at the scene a few years ago? He turned up in my group on release?' Katie nodded

190

sympathetically. It was hard in their line of work. Some of their colleagues would say good riddance, but Katie and Tom both let their emotions and human side encroach on their professional life at times. It was hard not to when you worked with the same people day in, day out. The cells, and often the prison gates, were just revolving doors. Of course, they both appreciated that some people were rotten to the core, probably born that way. There were others, though, who were not inherently bad. Frank was one of those. A bit of a bumbling idiot who couldn't seem to find his way back on track once the drink got hold of him. They saw it time and time again.

'I'm sorry,' said Katie, 'what happened?'

'They aren't sure yet. Looks like he fell or jumped; most likely he was so pissed, he fell over the edge.'

'Anything I can do?'

'I'm going to go tell his mum. I've met her before - she doesn't have any other close family and would appreciate it coming from me rather than a stranger who never met Frank. His bloody girlfriend only died the other week as well, an OD.'

'Let me know when you are on the way back, and I will stick the kettle on. I'm here catching up on admin for a few hours.'

Tom headed out of the station to pay a visit to Frank's mum. The sooner he could get there, the better, as the media were already reporting a body being found on The Hoe. It wouldn't take long for them to get hold of Frank's name and put the pieces together. The poor man was hounded enough in life and was unlikely to get any respite once his past offending was connected to the body found. The press didn't think of the family; Frank's mum had been through enough, and the least he could do was get there and make sure she heard it from him rather than the media. As he got in the car, he sent a quick text to Katie asking if she could get a VLO assigned to support Frank's mum through the identification process and help with the press. He then called Probation, asking to be put through to Anna to update her as he made the journey.

'I only said jokingly to Katie the other week that it seems as if someone has it in for Plymouth residents, but if I didn't know better, I really would think someone really was out there bumping off our regulars,' he joked. Anna chuckled, and Tom saw an opportunity to ask her if she fancied a drink one night. She gave a light laugh leaving Tom unclear if a drink was on the cards or not, and rang off, saying she needed to get her notes up to date.

Following her call with Tom, Anna added notes to Frank's file and sighed. She tapped out an email to Emma, Kylie, and Sally, copying Tom in, informing them that the body found looked to be Franks, but formal identification hadn't taken place yet. She started going back over her notes to make sure everything was up to date and she hadn't missed anything. The coroner would likely look through any content detailing conversations around suicidal thoughts with a fine-tooth comb. It was so unfair how the professionals got dragged through the mill any time anything happened with anyone on their radar – regardless of if it was a death, an overdose, or a further crime. The first place everyone looked to place blame or accountability was the professional services - the police and probation always seemed to be in the firing line these days.

Tom hesitated before ringing the doorbell at Frank's Mum's. The poor woman. It got no easier telling the next of kin that their loved one had been in an accident or was deceased, especially when it was a parent. He filled her in on the few facts he could give her. Frank's body was found on the rocks. They were not sure yet how long it had been there, but it was high enough on the rocks that it was not reached by the tide. Tom had been told it could have been there for some hours as it wasn't easy to spot from the street above. A group of paddle boarders had seen him and called 999. She would need to formally identify the body, but the description matched Frank, and his wallet was found on the body. He thought the woman had enough grief from her son's actions over the years and hoped she might finally get some peace. Though he knew she would never be at peace again. How do you recover from losing a child? She had answered the door with a resigned face when she saw who it was. She had accepted the news with quiet reservation, and her face did not betray the emotion he could see behind her eyes. He let her know it would not be him dealing with the case, but he wanted to let her know as he had known Frank. She thanked him, squeezing his hand, not letting go. Tom suggested she prepare herself for media interest but said a VLO would help with whatever she needed next. She said very little and declined the offer of Tom calling someone to come and be with her.

Tom gave his mum a call on the way back to the station and made a mental note to do so more often. She didn't live in Plymouth, and he must make more effort to get up to Gloucester to visit her. He sighed, he might not be a drunk like Frank was, but he knew his mum would still be disappointed in his behaviour. She loved his wife.

Arthur

Arthur was getting used to life outside again. Luckily the common criminals in Plymouth seemed to create enough headlines of their own that meant Arthur got a bit of respite from the media and local community. He enjoyed having his grandchildren around. He always loved having children around the place laughing and playing. The sound of their laughter gave him a renewed zest for life. He wasn't allowed to be left alone with them, but he didn't mind that so much. He was getting older, and running around after little ones was a young man's game. His wife was upset that she wasn't trusted to have the kids visit with Arthur there, but it suited him on the occasions his daughter was busy as he could go out for a couple of hours while his wife spent time with the kids. It gave Arthur a chance to go out and catch up with old friends with no one pestering him about where he was going. He knew they meant well, but it was stifling sometimes. He enjoyed reconnecting with old friends and getting back out on the golf course. They had quite the social life before all this business happened, and he hoped they could get this back, along with other parts of his life he missed.

Arthur's friends, Brian and Martha, had their grandson living with them now. The old photos in their hallway took him back, bringing up memories of the good old days. They had such fun, holidays together, and parties for the kids when they were younger. He remembered the boy's mother; she was always trouble. She used to knock about with his daughter until they fell out after the girl started making trouble for him. Her son, Dylan, didn't seem to be much better. He had a look of trouble about him and needed a firm hand to keep him out of trouble. His mother was the same; she was always putting herself out there. With her, it was all short skirts and flirting with everyone. As soon as he gave her what she was asking for, she backtracked, started making up stories. She made him out to be a monster. Young girls didn't realise the damage they could do, tarting themselves up and leading men on, then deciding that they didn't want it afterwards. That was years ago, long before the others who got him put away. Turned out Dylan's mum ended up with the life she deserved, turning to drugs and drink, barely speaking to her parents after they refused to believe her lies about Arthur.

'Why don't you both come over for dinner at the weekend?' Arthur said to Brian, 'The boy will be fine; he is old enough to look after himself for the evening. It sounds as though he had to when his mother was alive, anyway.' Arthur couldn't resist the dig. Martha looked stricken at the mention of Dylan's mum, and Arthur put his hand over hers in comfort. He always knew the right thing to say or do; it was how he always got what he wanted over the years. Until the unfortunate situation with his sentencing – he was lucky that his older friends like Brian and Martha stood by him, along with his wife and daughter. He headed home with a spring in his ageing step. Things were getting back on track. He had a new computer, was online and in touch with some old contacts, and also lots of new ones he had made in prison. Life was good.

Marie

Beth paid a surprise visit to Marie earlier that day, and now she was feeling subdued. Beth asked all sorts of questions about her relationship with John, about how they had met, how he was with the girls, did he ever look after them when she wasn't around. Marie felt unsettled, but Beth said it was routine when there was a new relationship. They wanted to make sure the girls were coping and their emotions were being adequately supported and managed. She asked so many questions that Marie couldn't help but feel there was more to it. Beth asked her to call if there was ever anything she wanted to talk about or if she ever had any concerns. When she spoke about John, she had nothing but praise for his relationship with the girls – she couldn't fault him and said he was the father they never had when Carl was alive. Alice had been a little quiet lately, but Marie put this down to her being content and settled. She was no longer hearing shouting and door slamming. She got on really well with John and had become a bit of a Daddy's girl with him. She finally had the stable home life she should have always had. Marie was torn away from her thoughts when she heard John come in the front door. He brought with him a large bouquet of flowers and a big bag of snacks and sweet treats. He pulled her to her feet and swept her up into his arms.

'What's got you in such a good mood?' Marie asked.

'I'm just in a good mood and pleased to see my wonderful, gorgeous, yummy mummy of a girlfriend,' John replied, giving her a kiss and a playful tap on the bum. 'Where are my favourite little munchkins? I bought snacks and thought we could put on a film and have a sofa picnic, and then perhaps I could have a grown-up sleepover with you,' he said, waggling his eyebrows jokily, then giving Marie a mock seductive look. All previous thoughts were wiped from her mind, and Marie called the girls down to choose a film while she hurried upstairs to straighten up the bedroom. She left John to supervise, forgetting that she had intended to have a chat with him about the visit from Beth earlier.

The
Professionals

'How did you get on with Marie?' Katie asked Beth, offering her a brownie from the box she brought with her.

'Sang his praises, as they always do.' Beth filled Katie in on the visit and said Marie was clearly in the honeymoon period where John could do no wrong. They always seem to go 'all in' so quickly. There was no evidence to say that he was a risk, but she had the same gut instinct that Katie did. There was nothing either of them could put their finger on with this case; it just didn't quite feel right. Katie had spoken to John at work the same day Beth spoke with Marie. John answered the questions about his ex-girlfriend and her children with textbook answers. He said he had been upset when the relationship ended, and perhaps he could have handled it better. He had clearly gone away from the chat with Katie feeling that he had given the right answers and passed some sort of test. She could see that look in his eyes where he thought he'd won and was trying to suppress a grin as she said goodbye. She had met enough bad eggs in her line of work to spot the red flags. The frustrating thing was that none of them could pinpoint anything specific.

'I guess all we can do is wait and see how it pans out,' Katie said.

~

Tom was at the probation office again. Anna was like forbidden fruit to him. She was resistant to his charms, and it made him want her all the more. As he pulled up a chair near her desk under the guise of popping in for a catch-up, he saw Jenna at her desk across the office.

'I know it's hard not to fall in love with me,' he said to Anna, plonking his mug of tea on her desk, 'so I just wanted to make sure you didn't get withdrawal from not seeing me at the group anymore.'

Anna laughed, picked up his mug and slipped a coaster underneath. 'I don't really have any updates for you,' she said, 'my little cherubs seem to be behaving. And, more importantly, since Frank's death, staying alive! Oh, actually, on that note, do you have an update on the chap in a coma after that poisoning or whatever happened down at the car park?' Tom tapped a quick text out to a nurse he had a thing with a few years ago. She was always helpful when he needed hospital updates and said he would let Anna know when he had any news. His phone buzzed with the response and message that he was still in a coma and was not expected to wake up. The hospital was in discussions with next of kin about turning off the life support.

'What did you just say about your little cherubs staying alive?' Tom joked.

'Ah, that one's not on my caseload, but I'll pass it on to his probation officer to keep her in the loop.' Tom noted Anna's dismissive tone as she turned back to the computer. He slurped down the rest of his tea, sent a flirty reply to the nurse and headed for the station.

~

'How long has it been going on?' said Jenna with a slightly raised and somewhat squeaky tone.

'What?' said Anna baffled.

'You and Tom.'

Anna laughed, 'absolutely not. Do I look stupid enough to fall for his narcissistic charms?!' she stopped herself as she saw the stricken look on Jenna's face and put a hand on her arm. 'You aren't to blame,' she reassured her, 'Men like him are all the same, preying on vulnerable women and casting them aside when they've got what they wanted. You had a lucky escape.'

Jenna didn't give up that easily and said it looked like they were more than friends, but her tone had lost its edge.

'Honestly, I'd never do that to you, and I would never look twice at a man like that anyway,' said Anna. Anna frowned, worrying about Jenna. She didn't seem to be settling back at work and had a distant air about her. 'Why don't we have a pizza night at mine? I'll see if some of the others fancy it, and we can have a good old-fashioned girls' night.'

~

Kylie was going through the candidates for the next group. She had long given up on being accepted into the 'in crowd' at the office and was sitting alone at her desk eating her lunch. The others were sitting in the lunchroom together, but they made no attempt to make space for her or make conversation when she got her lunch from the fridge, so she quietly left the room again. The next group candidates looked okay; there were no issues so far as she went through the risk assessments. She had heard of a couple of them who had been in and out of the system over the years, and as usual, one or two new faces. There were two that she just needed to check out with probation to see what their thoughts were on them being in the same group, and they had been co-defendants in a previous offence. She sent an email to Grace at probation to check, just as a message came in from Anna with the subject 'Pizza.' It made her feel a bit better about being left out in the office, and she gratefully accepted the invite to pizza night at Anna's. She glanced at her watch and sent a text to Bernie, reminding her she had a one-to-one later that afternoon to review her methadone script. There would be no reason to make any changes; Bernie always did what she was asked and was one of the easy ones to work with.

Bernie

Bernie watched from the window, a weird feeling in her stomach, adrenaline making her heart beat a little faster as she saw the cars pull up outside. She was at Jackie's cleaning when she noticed the cars arriving. There was one plain car with two smart looking plain clothes officers, and two patrol cans with six further officers, this time in uniform, all heading for the house next door. She watched carefully, slightly out of view but near enough to the window to see the door being answered and warrant cards flashed. She couldn't hear what was being said, but they had all trundled into the property, apart from one of the uniformed officers who had been left stationed outside the front door. Jackie was out shopping, so she had no one to watch and speculate with. She looked at James' closed door, itching to tell someone, even if he gave her the willies. It opened, causing the hairs on the back of her neck to stand on end. It was as if he had a sixth sense, knowing when she was outside his door. She looked past him as he opened the door and saw what looked like a naked person on his screen. Dirty bastard in there watching porn all day. Bernie told him the police were next door before resuming her observation post at the window. The officer was still standing guard, and there were no other signs of movement. James peered out, his face pale, and gruffly said he was going out. He disappeared into his room for a short period, and she could hear drawers and cupboards opening and slamming in a hurry before he left with his backpack via the kitchen side door. James forgot to lock his door in his haste to leave. Bernie glanced around and then over the banister quickly before pushing his door open. Her heart pounded in her chest. The screen she glimpsed earlier was now blank with a plain windows background, and there was an empty space where it looked like a laptop had been. The bottom drawer of the desk was open and empty. She pushed it closed out of habit and turned to leave the room. Something caught her eye as she turned. She stooped and picked up a USB stick. She surreptitiously slipped it into her pocket, hastily retreating and pulling the door closed behind her. She put the stick in the side pocket of her bag, grabbed the notepad from the fridge and scribbled a note to Jackie saying she was unwell and would finish the house tomorrow before locking the door and hurrying away. She glanced at her phone as she sat at the bus stop - she had enough time to visit the computer suite in the local library on the way to her appointment with Kylie if she hurried. She put her hand in her bag to ensure the USB stick was still there before boarding the bus.

Luke

Luke was nervous as he put on his suit jacket. He didn't know why he felt he had to get dressed up. Tilly's parents already hated him, so why did he care what they thought of him and what he wore? He was getting ready to attend her 18th birthday party. Her parents had hired a function room in a local hotel, and she said there were around 60 of her friends and family attending the buffet and party. Her parents wanted to take her, so he was meeting her there. There was a big easel-style sign in the hotel foyer with a baby photo of Tilly and an arrow pointing to the party's location. This was not Luke's world; he hesitated before going in, feeling out of place. He spotted Tilly talking to some people at the other side of the room and pushed himself to join the beginning of the party. He recognised a few people from the school. There was a table just inside the door where people were leaving presents and another long table set up ready for the buffet. The room had its own bar, with a sign reminding partygoers to have their ID ready and that drinks would be limited to one at a time. Luke rolled his eyes and ordered a drink before pointing to Tilly and persuading the barman to let him buy his girlfriend a birthday drink. It didn't take much persuasion, even out of his environment, others knew not to refuse a request from Luke.

The music was low, the DJ still setting up, but the room was filling quickly as people arrived. The present table was loaded, and Tilly's Dad looked anxious, fiddling with a microphone near the DJ booth. Luke made his way towards Tilly and handed her the drink whilst leaning in to give her a peck on the cheek.

'You look incredible,' he said, looking her up and down and taking in the shimmering dress that hugged her in all the right places. She wrapped her arms around his neck, pulling him in for a kiss that went on much longer than he expected. Her lips tasted sweet like cocktails, and she had clearly had a few drinks already. He pulled away, murmuring that there would be time for that later, but he wanted to meet her family. He doubted any of her family would be his biggest fans, given that her mother had probably already warned them about him, but he wanted to make the best impression he could. Tilly grabbed his hand and dragged him towards her dad for a formal introduction. It went better than Luke expected, and he let himself be swept off to meet her grandmother and some other relatives before she left him with some of her friends to go to the loo.

On her return, Tilly's dad gave a speech and shared memories of her childhood. Luke suddenly felt even more out of place. He hadn't had a family like this, no family parties, no dad to tell him he was proud of him or make a speech. His mum tried her best, but Luke felt annoyed with her. He was annoyed that she couldn't have stopped his dad from leaving, been a better wife and made him want to stay. He suddenly saw his life through the eyes of others, the eyes of people who didn't make their living through drugs and prostitutes and felt sick. How could he bring his beautiful, untarnished Tilly into this tainted world of his? Who was he kidding; he wasn't good enough for her. Now he had seen this clearly, he couldn't get out of there quick enough. He stumbled towards the doors, leaving his drink on the table by the presents. He pulled out his phone as he left the hotel, sending a text to Tilly, *I'm sorry, I just can't be here.* He turned his phone off and went to his mum's. As she opened the familiar front door to his childhood home, his anger dissolved, and suddenly he was the little boy without a dad, who just wanted a hug from his mum. Jackie pulled him in for an embrace soothing him, misinterpreting his hurt as a fallout with Tilly.

The next day, Luke woke up in his childhood bedroom. It had been redecorated since he had grown up there, but it was still his room. It was still a place he would always feel safe. Downstairs he found his mum bustling in the kitchen making pancakes. He couldn't remember the last time he had pancakes. He laughed as he saw his mum was not just making any pancakes, but happy face pancakes. She set the table for the three of them like old times.

'There will be other girls, girls who appreciate you,' she said, still assuming that Tilly had broken up with him. James joined them, and for a brief period, time had frozen, and they were two little boys back at the kitchen table having happy face pancakes made by their doting mum. Forgotten were the times they had to fend for themselves while she sat on the sofa crying. They were transported back to the good memories. The spell was broken when Bernie arrived to clean. Jackie made her a cup of coffee and told her to sit down and have a drink before she got started. Luke drank his coffee as he listened to Bernie and his mum speculating about what the police wanted with the neighbours. Evidently, Bernie saw the police arrive, and his mum saw them leaving with boxes, hours later. The neighbours went with the police for a couple of hours but were back in the house now, and no one was any the wiser about what had happened.

'I'll ask around, Mum, do a bit of digging. I can always go and bang on the door and ask them outright if I don't hear anything. We don't want trouble on your doorstep.' Luke finally looked at his phone to find missed calls and messages from Tilly. He felt shame at his behaviour. He saw her family, a normal family who cared about each other, with a mum and a dad who provided for their children. He loved his mum, but if he hadn't stepped up when he was too young, he and his brother would probably have ended up in care. He didn't have the childhood that Tilly had, and he didn't want to bring her any further into his world. He sent her a message apologising and said she deserves someone better than him and it's best to stop things now. His phone immediately rang. Luke stared at it ringing in his hand until it stopped. It rang again. Luke switched it to silent and put it in his pocket.

'Right, Mum, I am off, places to go, people to see,' he said giving her a hug.

~

Luke cleared the missed calls from Tilly and deleted her messages without reading them. His phone vibrated in his hand, and Bernie's name flashed up on the screen. Tilly was at Docker Street, drunk and shouting the odds. Bernie was trying to calm the girl down and take her to the safe flat nearby, but Luke could hear Tilly in the background, refusing to listen until Luke was there. He sighed. It wasn't good for business to be drawing attention to Docker Street. He didn't need the police turning up because Tilly was upsetting people.

Her

Things had been quiet since Frank's death. She was quite fond of the old bugger, so it didn't give her any joy to do what needed to be done. He was frustrating and didn't help himself, but he was also a very sad and lonely individual. Like many others, he wasn't a bad person, he just made so many bad choices that he couldn't be allowed to continue ruining other people's lives. They always had an opportunity to change before she took the decision out of their hands, and they never seemed to take it.

She thought back over the years, trying to think of someone who had actually changed for the better and stopped hurting others. Anyone she thought of had ended up back in the system in some way or another – even if they did sort themselves out for a period of time, they soon came back, causing trouble again. Often, if they were off the radar for a while, presumed to be doing okay, they had an almighty relapse and ended up dead anyway. Some came back reincarnated as drug workers. The annoying ones that always thought they knew best. Their help for others wasn't pure - it was still selfish as the only way they could stay on track was to surround themselves with other people who become projects to 'fix up'. They were not really 'cured' or free; their recovery was now paid employment and the only way to stay clean was to stay in that world, never free to move on. Yes, staff that were reformed characters were the most annoying of all. Unfortunately, they weren't usually hurting anyone, so nothing would be gained by getting rid of any of them.

~

She had pizza night with the girls coming up to look forward to and would enjoy getting the news on what they had been up to, and gossip on some of the regulars. It wasn't all shop talk at the socials, but it was a handy way to catch up and have frank discussions about the regulars away from the desks and listening ears. She wanted to get everyone else's take on the Marie situation. Every time she ran past her house these days, John was there. It appears he had his feet well and truly under the table. Had he officially moved in? That would need to be checked out. She wasn't sure what to do about this situation. Marie was not an offender or a substance user herself. However, she had been given a chance to change and put those kids first, and had royally fucked it up if it turned out John was a paedo. Not that there was any evidence of this, but questions were being asked. Something was causing suspicion; they just didn't know what yet. Marie had let him into her home so quickly. Of course, we never really know another person, but she hadn't even attempted to do any due diligence before exposing those poor girls to God knows what. There was no proof, no evidence. Whilst it was all hearsay, she would continue to mull it over. What to do if it turned out he was up to something? Marie couldn't be allowed to continue to put them at risk, but then she couldn't leave those girls without a parent. Oh god, she would be responsible for orphaning them, but surely then they would have a chance to find a home where they were safe. They deserved to be safe, but how many 'safe' homes turned out to be risky? This was a minefield. She was too new to all this to be navigating this kind of decision-making. The others had all been black and white decisions, with a bit of opportunism thrown in to make things happen. She wanted her actions to be for the greater good, she was saving people, but she was starting to see the weight her decisions carried. This was another one of those times where she craved a partner – in life, and in deciding who should be sacrificed.

The
Professionals

Katie felt as though there was something in the air in Plymouth. She couldn't quite put her finger on it, but there was something sinister going on. There were too many little things that didn't quite add up yet. There was the situation with John and Marie and her girls. Then there was his ex-girlfriend, who seemed genuine, but there was no evidence for any of this. Was it a coincidence that Arthur had been recently released from prison? Then there was the raid the other day. They had seized all the computers and technology of a convicted sex offender, but nothing was found. The man had been convicted of two rapes nearly 15 years ago, and his record had been clean since his release. There was a hit on a website with an IP address registered at his address. Someone had put two and two together and come up with five. The website in question was children, so unlikely to be the same perpetrator as it didn't fit with his MO. She knew it had to be followed up, but it meant that the real sicko was still out there. The address housing the actual offender had to be close for the IP address to have taken them there. The real offender could even have been watching the raid. The house they raided was next door to Luke's mum. He was well known to them, but for all his scoundrel-like tendencies, Luke had a line he didn't cross, and was not into children. She doubted if he even knew there was a convicted sex offender next door; he wouldn't be happy about it. It was a long time ago, and the guy had relocated Plymouth, so his name wasn't known locally. Otherwise, no doubt, there would have been some sort of ruckus.

~

'It's ridiculous,' said Jenna to Grace. She had finished the counselling sessions the doctor had referred her for and now had to apply for more. The waiting list was 18 months long. 'How is anyone supposed to get help or attempt to move on with their lives?!'

Grace understood, 'The trouble is, you have a job and some stability, which pushes you down the list. It is bad enough trying to get help for the offenders, let alone someone who hasn't hit their ridiculous criteria of being at rock bottom to get bumped up the list.' As she said it, she thought Jenna probably was close to rock bottom but voicing that wouldn't do any good. 'You could always go to Revive and see if you can get some support through them,' she mused, trying to help. The trouble was that most of their offenders and clientele went there; it was so difficult to find confidential support when you worked in this world. If Jenna was seen there or attended any support groups there, it would be gossiped about in probation groups, and her confidentiality had zero chance of being respected.

~

Girl's night at Anna's had finally arrived and couldn't come soon enough for some of the gang. It had been a while since they had all got together outside of work. It was usually quick trips to Costa before or after mutual appointments. Jenna was in remarkably good spirits, and everyone was pleasantly surprised that she seemed to be turning a corner. Beth had the usual joviality of someone who had the night off being a parent and had turned up with a bottle of wine declaring, 'mums' night off!' Anna thought Kylie always seemed so grateful to be included – it was a bit sad, really. The girl was a little odd and just didn't seem to make friends. She was nice enough, and they all got on, but there was always an air of gratitude for any attention she received.

'Any new men on the horizon, girls?' asked Sally to a chorus of responses that indicated no-one could be bothered with dating. Everyone left smiling and merry after the catch-up. Kylie had appointed herself designated driver and dropped those who had been drinking home.

~

The next morning, Beth arrived at Dylan's parents' house as a car pulled away. The man looked familiar, but she couldn't quite place him. It reminded her of the photos in their hallway; it was the same person she couldn't quite place.

Beth had good news for Brian and Martha; it looked like everyone who had been involved in assessing them was going to be recommending that Dylan stay with them permanently. The school had submitted a report saying that, whilst Dylan had a long way to go emotionally, it was clear his immediate needs were being met. He looked healthier, despite the grief and loss of his mother, and was engaging a lot better. Beth put this down to the home-cooked meals and stable life with his grandparents offered him. They were pleased with the news, and they all agreed that they just needed to continue as they were until the court date was set for the final recommendation. On the way out, Beth saw the photo again in the hallway and asked if the man was someone well known as she thought she recognised him. Dylan's grandmother, Martha, hesitated before saying that he used to be their daughter's Head Teacher and was an old friend of theirs. She paused again before saying; he had been away and had recently got back in touch now he was back in the area.

Luke

Following the debacle where Tilly turned up drunk at Docker Street, Luke and Tilly talked things through. He still wasn't convinced that it was the right thing to stay together, but she was insistent that she knew what she was getting into and that she didn't mind that he wasn't always a good guy. He couldn't shake the feeling that he would break her, that he didn't deserve her after the things he had done, and the life he chose to lead. Tilly pointed out that she was far from innocent when he met her.

Something Tilly said when she was drunk played on Luke's mind - she said he wouldn't want to know her if he knew what she had done. When he asked her the next day, she said she couldn't remember, that it couldn't have been important. This was not the first time she had alluded to something she ended up brushing off.

Things were back on track with plans to meet Luke's Mum, who seemed to be going all out as if the late Queen Elizabeth herself was coming for tea. Tilly arrived at Luke's ready to go to his mum's, wearing a knee-length lacy white dress. Luke had never seen her looking so demure. The white dress gave off an almost bridal vibe, and he found himself picturing her waiting for him at an altar. He shook his head, wondering where those thoughts had come from. Marriage was not something he had ever wanted. His parent's marriage planted the seed that marriage didn't end in happiness from a young age, and he grew up believing that relationships never ended well. He had seen enough married men (and the occasional woman) down on Docker Street looking for prostitutes, that his experiences as an adult only compounded the beliefs that were ingrained in him when his father walked out on them. The smell of his mum's cooking hit them as Jackie opened the door in greeting. She immediately enveloped Tilly in a hug and stepped back, exclaiming what a pretty thing she was, all memory of her comments about Luke finding someone better forgotten. She showed them into the living room, and Luke noticed fresh flowers on the table and the candles that were usually saved for best had been lit. Luke was sent to get drinks, and his mum was leading Tilly towards family photos. The evening went well, and Luke was happy to see the only women he had ever really cared for getting along.

Bernie

Jackie gave Bernie the rundown of the night before, and Bernie smiled, pleased to hear it went well. A different version of Tilly appeared to have attended to meet Jackie than the one who was drunkenly shouting and making a scene when Bernie met her. Bernie smiled, seeing Jackie happy; their friendship had blossomed in the short time since they met, and they increasingly confided in each other. After their catch-up, Jackie had gone into town, and Bernie was busying around. The sun created warm patches on the carpet, and Bernie opened the windows letting the fresh air fill the house. She pushed open the landing window and saw James standing in the garden, his phone pressed to his ear. He paced as he spoke. She moved closer to the open window, gently pushing it open a little wider.

'If anyone found it, we'd know by now,' he said, 'you know you can trust me. This was one mistake. I was spooked by the police next door.' Bernie's forehead wrinkled. She thought of the USB stick still in her handbag. The IT suite at the library had been closed for maintenance when she went, and she had since forgotten about it. James ran his hand through his hair, his hushed tone becoming more intense as he rubbed his forehead, trying to reassure whoever he was speaking to.

Bernie's fingernails dug into her hands as she clenched her fists, her heart racing. *Should she hand the USB stick to the police? What if it was just James' college coursework?* Maybe she was being silly. Bernie couldn't shake the bad feeling whenever she saw or thought of James. *Could she hand the USB stick in if she didn't like what she saw?* In her world, they didn't grass, but Bernie had a feeling she was about to learn where her line was. She had to find out. Bernie finished running the hoover around downstairs and wiped over the kitchen work surfaces in time to catch the bus to the library. She was pleased to see the IT suite was open, and she found a computer in the corner, surreptitiously eyeing the other library users for any sign they were paying her attention. She felt like she had a neon sign above her head and a bomb in her bag. Bernie took a deep breath and pushed the USB stick into the port, clicking on the drive to open it and view its contents. She felt as if her actions were happening in slow motion. As the icon spun around, waiting for it to open, it suddenly occurred to her it might have a password. *Of course, it would if it was as important as it seemed to be.* A box appeared on the screen with the contents of the USB stick ready to access. She clicked on the first image and saw a picture of a little blonde girl smiling, then another with the same girl. As she clicked through the photos, it appeared like a family photo album; only it didn't feel right. The photos changed, and some of them looked like they were taken from afar, in a park. Bernie kept moving through the photos, her heart still racing. There was another folder on the drive, she clicked on it, and it asked for a password. She removed the stick and reinserted it, trying again. She didn't know what that would do, but she tried again out of frustration. She opened a browser tab and typed 'How to open a folder on USB stick without the password.' Google offered several articles and links, the words 'bitLocker,' 'decrypt', and 'recovery key' swam

218

around in front of her. She sighed, rubbing her temples. Bernie looked at the photos again, picking out six or seven different children. The little blonde girl she had first seen appeared to be a twin, as there were smiling photos of the two of them together. It struck her as weird that there were no photos with their parents. Something still felt wrong, but she didn't know what to do next. Bernie pulled the stick out of the computer and put it back in her bag. She couldn't talk about it with Jackie, but she wasn't sure who to ask.

The
Professionals

The phone rang constantly, and emails were piling up. There were a few people off on long-term sick, and the probation service was stretched. People were always off sick, but instead of looking at why or addressing the problems, management kept their heads down. Anna, Grace and their colleagues were busy picking up the slack.

'Have you heard from Jenna?' Grace asked.

'Not since pizza night, I did message her a couple of days ago checking in, but I haven't heard back.'

'I'll put a message in the WhatsApp group.' The message quickly showed as read by a few people. Some responded, saying they hadn't heard from her. Anna checked the private message she had seen a few days ago, seeing that it had been delivered but not read. Ominous thoughts squirmed at the back of her mind, her stomach feeling unsettled. 'I'll drive over to hers at lunchtime and check in,' she said.

Anna sat in the car and took a deep breath before crossing the road to ring Jenna's doorbell. She hovered, trying again. I'm sure it's nothing, she thought, trying unsuccessfully to stop the unease in her stomach from growing as her pulse quickened. She pressed the bell again before hammering on the door and shouting through the letterbox. She could see a pile of post on the doormat. Something wasn't right. Anna pulled out her mobile, scrolling through the phonebook to find Katie's number. Katie heard the fear in Anna's voice. She pressed the button to activate the lights and siren and pulled up in a patrol car within minutes. It felt like hours to Anna. Katie tried the door before telling Anna to step back and kicking it in. The air escaping the flat swirled around them with the rich odour of rotting meat. The sweet undertones wafting out as if an afterthought. Katie pressed the button on her radio, her shaky voice advising the control room that entry had been forced. Katie's training took over as she noticed the key in the door, locking it from the inside. The door was undamaged, and no visible windows appeared broken or forced. Her pulse was beating faster as she felt the surge of adrenaline racing through her body. They moved from room to room methodically looking for their friend, Katie noting no signs of a break-in. Katie pushed open the bedroom door and stumbled, taking a step back into Anna. Anna didn't move - her mouth open and unblinking eyes staring into the room. It didn't matter how many deaths Katie attended, it never got easier. Katie looked around the room – there were no immediate signs of a struggle or any other person having been there. Her eyes travelled up to the ornate Victorian light fitting, taking in the small cracks in the ceiling rose where the plaster had reacted to the strain. She let her eyes follow the line of the ligature to Jenna's neck, stretched by the weight of her body. The ligature had cut into her neck, and there was a trickle of blood against her pale skin. Her eyes were wide open, staring, and there was a dark burgundy red colour visible where blood had pooled in her hands and feet. Below Jenna's feet was a chair from the dining table lying on its side. They stepped outside, filling their lungs with fresh air. Katie radioed for backup. Anna's hand shook as she unlocked her car and pulled a bottle of water from her bag. She gulped the water, trying to wash away the taste in her mouth. It lingered like garlic the morning after.

'Are you okay?' Katie asked, putting her hand on Anna's arm. Katie was shaken herself; it was different when it was someone she knew. They didn't need to speak to agree that there was little point in attempting to get Jenna's body down. The smell told them that life had left her body, replaced with the steady process of decomposition.

Katie's phone rang and as she pulled it out of her pocket, they both saw Tom's name on the screen.

'Not now, Tom,' she answered.

'Is it her?'

'Yes,' she replied, her teeth clenched and hung up.

Katie sank into her desk chair, struggling to keep her eyes open. Anna and her had given separate statements as to why they had attended Jenna's flat. She had spoken about Jenna's mental state. The last time either of them had seen her had been when they were all together at pizza night. Katie had been asked if Jenna had a partner. She didn't know what to do about Tom. She just said that she didn't think Jenna was seeing anyone, which was true. She had trembled as she said it. She knew she should have mentioned the affair with Tom. She had lied by omission. She wanted to ask how Anna was, but Anna had gone when Katie had finished giving her statement. She grabbed her phone typing, 'wine later?' getting a response almost instantly, 'yes, I'll be home for the evening by 7 pm, come anytime.' Tom sat in his chair at the desk next to her, watching her.

'Just don't,' she said.

'I'm allowed to care.'

'You didn't care before about your wife, your reputation or Jenna's feelings! When are you going to grow up and stop treating women like toys you can pick up and put down?!' hissed Katie, her voice low and monotone. She grabbed her bag, jabbed at the button to shut down her computer and stomped out. Katie and Tom never argued, not properly. He would usually be the first person she went to with work stuff, but today she just couldn't. Jenna had her demons, but right now, Katie wanted someone to blame.

Katie and Anna didn't say much over the wine. Just being together was enough. They discussed telling their colleagues and decided that they'd rather they hear it from them than in the news. Jenna's parents would have been informed by now. They carefully composed a message and sent it to the WhatsApp group.

Her (then)

She took her mum a cup of coffee and two buttery slices of toast in bed, giving her a kiss goodbye and headed to school. It was like any other morning.

A keen student, she didn't skip classes like some of her peers, and attended all her lessons. She enjoyed English – the power of the written word and how meaning can be communicated or twisted at the writer's leisure and the reader's pleasure. She didn't know yet what she wanted to do with her life, but by now had been supporting her mum through the low periods for a few years and thought she might like to do something where she could help people. It was like any other school day.

She strolled home from school, her headphones over her ears, listening to her CD player. She smiled as she passed familiar gardens and flowers that reminded her of when her mother used to walk her to school. Throwing her school bag on the sofa, she opened the fridge looking for inspiration. Her eyes settled on a jar of peanut butter and she popped two slices of toast in the toaster and went in search of her mum. As she took her headphones off, the silence in the house enveloped her. Her mum would usually be pottering around or watching TV in the afternoons. The TV was silent. She frowned, calling out for her mum. She pushed open the bedroom door and saw the toast she had taken in before school on the bedside table, the full cup of coffee next to it. The bed was made.

Her stomach fluttered - a message to her brain. She rubbed the back of her neck, puzzled and called out again, stepping onto the landing. The bathroom door was closed. She hesitated, her skin tingled, ears straining for a sound, any sound. As she pushed the handle down and opened the door, she saw the little stool she used to stand on to reach the sink. It was on its side. Memories flashed through her mind, her mum helping her to stand on it and brush her teeth, her mum sitting on it to comb conditioner through her hair, the time she climbed on it and tried to reach the cabinet on her own and fell off it causing a huge lump on her forehead, where she hit it on the sink. Of course, she could reach things herself now she was bigger, but they kept it in the bathroom out of habit. Her mum used it to change the lightbulb on the landing. They say we have a gut instinct that knows when something bad is going to happen. In that moment, she focused on the stool, holding onto the memories, her gut told her not to look up. She tore her eyes from the stool and looked up. It was only as she did so that her brain registered the putrid odour. Her mother's face was devoid of colour. Her eyes stared into space, the whites tinged with red, and her neck stretched like a cartoon. She fled from the room, running out of the house and emptying the contents of her stomach in the front garden. She heaved again and again until there was nothing left to bring up. She vaguely registered the neighbour asking if she was okay before she ran.

Her (now)

She was transported back to the day she found her mother; the memories attacked her like a knife piercing her heart. She was sad, angry, upset, and regretful - every emotion under the sun. Her jaw clenched, and her brow knotted in a frown. She blamed herself, her colleagues, Tom. This was his fault. Jenna never got over their relationship ending. She never got over the loss of the baby. She blamed Jenna's manager at work, her counsellor, her friends. She blamed the offenders and clients, the addicts, and the scumbags taking up all the community resources. If they were not all overrun with these dregs of society, then good people would have more support. If they were not all busy being overworked with high caseloads, they might have noticed. None of them had checked in with Jenna. No one had said anything in the group chat since pizza night. She had been smiling that night, her eyes shining, sitting on the sofa with her feet up as she ate pizza and laughed with everyone. She said she was moving forward. Why had none of them noticed? They say people are happiest when they have decided to end their life, was that it? Had she decided, and not one of them noticed what was really going on. If they were not all so busy with work, their minds and compassion directed elsewhere, they might have had time to look after their own. She had a fire inside her, a renewed passion for finding the next people to permanently remove from their caseloads so they could do some actual work with people who deserved it. *Why was Jenna on an 18 month wait list for counselling when there were junkie prostitutes who got bumped up the list because their need was deemed greater?*

This was her mother all over again. Two gentle souls, destroyed by men, unable to get the help they needed due to the selfishness of others.

Marie

Marie made lists of everything John might need to know while she was away with her sister – emergency contacts, foods the girls liked and disliked, bedtimes. She wrote a list of things she needed to pack and got the laundry up to date. Marie hadn't been away on her own since before she had the girls, and now, she had two entire nights. She loved them, but she sometimes felt like she didn't know who she was anymore - besides being a mum and, previously, Carl's wife. John paid for a spa day for her and her sister, and she was looking forward to a day of ultimate relaxation. John was looking after the girls, and she smiled at the thought of them bonding and having a fun weekend. He spoilt them something rotten with ice creams, late bedtimes and games, but she didn't mind too much. They were good girls and deserved it after all they had been through. Marie added a new swimsuit to her list, along with pizzas and junk food as a treat. She reflected on the visit from Beth and Beth's observation that it had all moved quickly with John. Beth had asked how well Marie really knew him, but she had pointed out that he was Carl's friend, so it was all okay. Marie paused, clenching the pen between her teeth as she realised; she had never actually heard Carl speak about John. He might have mentioned him once or twice in reference to car sharing or as a colleague, but she couldn't remember specifics or even the mention of John joining Carl and his mates at the pub. She had met most of the usual crowd, in passing, at some point or other over the years. Beth was just being dramatic and planting bad seeds in her head, surely. Was it too soon to leave John alone with the girls all weekend? They always ran to John, begging him to take them to the park or play Barbies. Their relationship with Marie was strong, and she was sure if there was anything wrong, they would tell her. And she was so looking forward to this time away. Everything was fine when he looked after them other times, and she'd know if something was wrong, wouldn't she?

Bernie

Jackie began washing the lunch dishes while waiting for the kettle to boil. She sighed happily as she put her hand under the tap, letting the warm water run through her fingers. Luke was beside her, ready with the tea towel. Bernie cleared the table wearing an amused smile at the well-choreographed domestication between Luke and Jackie. Tilly sat at the table chattering away with them all, when Luke's phone rang. A few short words and he left Tilly with his mum and Bernie.

Bernie and Luke's relationship had taken on a whole new level since she had been working at his mum's, or was it since Tilly had been on the scene? Either way, Bernie could not believe this was the same man who had ordered for her fingers to be broken. How quickly the world around you can change, she mused. Jackie had welcomed her into the home, and she fitted in like a member of the family. Jackie made a pot of tea and waved a mug at Bernie, indicating for her to join Jackie and Tilly. Jackie beamed, showing off Tilly like a proud mother. Tilly was soon showing them pictures of her holiday last year at her family's villa in Turkey and saying they must join her next year. When Jackie excused herself to use the loo, Bernie seized the opportunity to ask Tilly about the USB stick.

'Funny story, and someone your age might help an old dinosaur like me,' she began, 'I have a USB stick, and I have only gone and forgotten my password. Do you know how I could get back into it?'

Tilly offered to take the stick and look and said she was sure Luke wouldn't mind looking if she couldn't get into it. Bernie immediately retracted, shakily saying she thought she might have suddenly remembered it. Maybe she should throw it away, she thought, but that nagging feeling was still there. Her phone flashed with a reminder of an appointment later with Kylie, and an idea formed. She'd wait until there was no one around and drop it somewhere, addressed to Kylie. That way, the decision was out of her hands and Kylie, or whoever found it could figure out what to do with it if anything. Kylie would know what the best thing to do with it would be, and knew the right people for if it was as sinister as Bernie's gut told her. Bernie let out a breath, feeling much better with the beginning of a plan. She reached into her bag and put her fingers around the stick, checking it was still there. The smooth plastic felt like it was burning her skin, its secrets trying to get out.

Tilly and Bernie never mentioned their meeting at Docker Street when Tilly was drunk and looking for Luke. Bernie wasn't sure if Tilly even remembered it or not. Tilly seemed perfectly pleasant now; however, Bernie felt like the wild child was still in there, hiding behind the perfectly polished persona Tilly presented to the world. That was the trouble with these rich girls, they always had a rebellious streak, and trouble was never far behind. She was pleased to see how happy Jackie and Luke were, but knew the girl would cause problems if she didn't get what she wanted.

The
Professionals

The mood was sombre across the services. Jenna might not have been known by everyone, but she was one of their own. Probation, police, Revive, Phoenix, housing services and rough sleepers' teams, Social Services, hostels – they all felt the loss. They all knew that it could have been any one of them. Whilst everyone has their own demons and battles to fight, they all shared the experience of working in this tough industry. Exactly what had pushed Jenna over the edge, they may ever know. The agencies might not always see eye to eye, but they were all spokes in the same wheel.

'How could none of us have noticed? What kind of shitty friends are we?' Emma asked Beth. 'I feel just awful that we all saw her last week, and none of us checked in since. None of us noticed that she had been quiet,' she continued.

'We all work with vulnerable people, women, for a living, and we can't even notice the signs in our own friend,' Beth agreed. Similar conversations were happening at the probation office, their colleagues in shock.

'I wonder when the clients will be told,' Emma speculated.

~

Anna skimmed through the email silently. 'God forbid they call some sort of meeting and offer support or compassion. Business as usual,' she ranted to no-one in particular. The email gave the brief details that Jenna had passed away with a link to The Samaritans website. Funeral details were to follow.

Grace looked up from her desk opposite Anna. She said nothing. They all had the same email. What was there to say?

~

Tom was quiet, pushing down the stirring of guilt he felt in his gut. His wife realised something was wrong when he told her that a colleague had passed away. She pursed her lips as she busied away in the kitchen. Tom felt uneasy, wincing as the plates were laid on the table noisily. The question hung in the air, unspoken.

'Perhaps, we could learn a lesson from this; life is precious,' Tom said, eventually breaking their silence and suggesting they have a family day at the weekend. He hovered near her, not quite touching, their eyes not meeting.

~

Kylie took the envelope, looking at her name on it, frowning. The Receptionist hadn't seen who dropped it off. Kylie sat at her desk and opened the envelope to see a USB stick. She plugged it into the computer and opened the file explorer to see what was on it. It looked like family photos. Why would this have been left for her? She scrolled through them, not seeing any way to identify them; there was no school uniform and no photos with adults or at landmarks. As she scrolled, it appeared odd that there seemed to be lots of pictures of different children taken in the same places. It didn't look like school or nursery photos. Kylie frowned and clicked on the last folder. It was locked. She was fairly savvy with computers, but didn't know how to get around the password. She wasn't sure what to do next, when Tom and Katie came in.

'Just passing and thought we would pop in,' Tom asserted. Kylie smiled, admiring his infectious grin. Clients were behaving a lot better since the police presence increased at the agency. She heard the same about the probation offices. The police were busy, but it really helped them out when they spent a bit more time there. The dealing outside had definitely reduced, and there had been a lot fewer incidents of drug use in the toilets.

'Good timing, something a bit weird just happened,' Kylie said, gesturing for Tom to pull a chair over, 'someone left a USB stick in reception for me.' She indicated the screen and the password locked files. 'The stick is just full of photos of children. I don't recognise any of them, so I have no idea why it's been sent to me. I don't know if it belongs to a school or a photographer; maybe you can trace it?' She passed him the wireless mouse as he leaned in, his aftershave cloying the surrounding air. She noticed his jaw clench as he clicked through the photos before closing it down and abruptly saying they would pass it to tech to have a look. Katie was loitering and passed him an evidence bag.

'Have you heard when Jenna's funeral is yet?' Tom asked, throwing the sealed bag back to Katie. Kylie shook her head, her eyes misting up.

~

Beth put her bag on the passenger seat and entered Dylan's grandparents' address in her satnav before pulling out of the car park. She was never confident of finding her way around that area. The court case was last week and his grandparents were granted custody of Dylan. She wanted to pay them a visit to say congratulations and check how they were settling in following the hearing. Martha indicated for her to go through to the lounge, where Dylan was sitting on the sofa, picking at his sleeve. He grunted in acknowledgement, not looking up when she asked how he was finding it, living with his grandparents.

'S'alright. Rather have my mum back, though,' he shrugged. As she brought in some freshly baked ginger cake for them all, Martha said she felt like they'd been given a second chance. A distant look passed across her face as she spoke about their strained relationship with Dylan's mum, describing her as a troublemaker. Dylan remained silent. Beth smiled at him sympathetically and nodded at the door, prompting him to shuffle off, muttering about homework.

'She even accused one of our friends of being inappropriate with her,' Martha continued, 'can you believe that?!' Beth froze, a sudden realisation hitting her like a blow to the gut. She realised who the man in the picture in the hallway was.

'Wait, your friend in the photos in the hallway, that's Arthur McIntyre? Arthur McIntyre, who has just been released from prison?'

Martha looked sheepish, 'Well, yes, I did tell you he had been away. Our Dylan's mum accused him of all sorts of awful things. He was like an uncle to her; it was wicked the things she said.'

'Does Dylan know?'

'I wouldn't have thought so, we aren't proud of her behaviour, so it isn't something that comes up in conversation. From what I can gather his mum never told him why we had the falling out, so I don't see any reason why she would have told him the things she made up about Arthur.' All sorts of thoughts were flying around in Beth's head, but she held them in, closing her mouth, not sure she could trust herself to speak.

She looked at her phone, 'I am so sorry, Martha, thank you for the lovely cake, but an emergency has just come in, and I must dash off. I will be in touch about a follow-up.' Beth rushed out of the door, leaving Martha staring after her. She got in the car, over-revving as she pulled away out of view of the house and put the handbrake on so she could send Emma a voice note pre-empting her return to the office.

'What the actual fuck?' Emma said incredulously, 'as if they didn't believe their own daughter and then let the dirty perve near their grandson. Some people shouldn't be allowed to be parents.'

'I know,' said Beth scooping the froth off her coffee with her finger.

Emma sighed, 'Although, aside from the whole, you know, noncing thing, no one spares a thought for the social workers and the paperwork this creates for us.'

'Emma!' exclaimed Beth. Emma was right, though. Beth needed to think about how to approach this and make sure her risk assessments and paperwork were thorough and up to date. She needed the press attention of social services letting an orphaned boy live with friends of a convicted paedophile, like a bullet to head.

Arthur

The world changed while Arthur was in prison - everything was now at his fingertips, and he could access whatever he wanted online. He had made contacts in prison who gave him the IT education that college wouldn't give you. Before he came to prison, he had only just got a computer. It had been very basic, and he hadn't ever got to grips with the old dial-up internet, let alone heard of the dark web. Prison was never going to be a nice experience, but at least he was able to meet some like-minded fellows to serve his sentence alongside. There were quite a few older gentlemen on his landing. They tended to put them all together. There were a few young ones, deemed too vulnerable to be with the main prison population due to the nature of their offences. These tended to be the ones who showed them how to use the computers on the wing. They had a mini computer suite. They weren't supposed to be left unsupervised, but with staffing shortages, the officers were never able to keep a very close eye on them. The computers weren't supposed to be able to access the internet, but somehow the youngsters had managed to bypass any security blocks to help Arthur get set up online. In return, he often helped out with paperwork and appeal processes.

Arthur's new computer sat in the living room, and he was often found looking at golfing sites. He encouraged his wife to use it, and occasionally, they looked up things to show the grandchildren when his daughter was visiting with them. He knew to make sure the history was filled with innocuous searches such as Peppa Pig or the UK's best golfing holidays. The speed and efficiency of the machine amazed him. He kept his laptop in the shed at the allotment. As he handed over the cash, he was informed that a dongle was all he needed to go with the laptop, and he would have the same internet access he had at home. He smiled and licked his lips. Arthur wasn't convicted of internet crimes; however, there had been some discussion over his licence conditions around computers and use of IT. He was told he must let the authorities know about any mobile phones, tablets, computers or laptops he had access to. Arthur didn't even know what a tablet was. He was told he is not allowed to delete his search history and must present any devices as requested for random checks. He hadn't declared the laptop in the allotment, or the pre-paid mobile phones. No-one knew about the area beneath the weed killer hollowed out of the compacted earth, perfect for storing things he didn't want to be found. His case had been high profile. When he first arrived in prison, people would shout at him on the wings or make comments. Some people avoided him. The prison officers were blunt and unhelpful, lacking the respect he was used to garnering from others. He was a professional, used to being respected, but in prison, the professionals treated him like a common criminal. Well, most of them. Not all of them were as professional as the uniform implied. This was how the dongles and mobile phones found their way onto the wings. They brought the drugs in as well, but Arthur wanted no part of that.

Arthur was initially at a prison a few hours from home, but after a few years, he moved to a prison closer to home. It was a difficult journey for his wife, so he was glad to see her more often after the move. He occasionally recognised students from his school – they still called him Sir. The media attention of his case helped him to nurture relationships with other prisoners who had similar predilections. They taught him about the internet; something Arthur had previously tried to avoid as the world progressed around him.

Arthur knew he needed to keep his social life going, be visible and be seen to be nothing more than an old retiree going about his days. He had made some useful contacts at the golf course. He needed the laughter and comradery that spending time with Brian and Martha afforded him. He missed that during his time 'away'. His wife enjoyed hosting dinners, and it was nice to see her with a sense of purpose. She bustled about in the kitchen with a spring in her step. That daughter of Brian's dying recently had been a relief. Their grandson, Dylan, didn't know what his mother accused Arthur of, or the lad would have been less amenable to Arthur visiting. He hoped Brian would convince the boy to join them on the golf course. Arthur's eyes lit up when Dylan was around. He had never had a particular type when it came to the students or young people he paid special attention to. He described it to his peers as a feeling he got when he saw potential that needed to be nurtured.

Arthur attended his appointment at probation, and a duty worker informed him he would no longer be seeing Jenna. The duty worker didn't even attempt to conceal his clock-watching, frequently looking down at a list on his clipboard. Arthur's appointments were usually longer, but the duty worker was clearly only concerned with it being a box ticking exercise. He pottered off to the allotment for some 'alone time'. His smile at the thought of his shed was soon replaced by a knot in his stomach as he recalled the missing USB stick. He had quickly picked up on the benefits of modern technology but was also realising the risks if things didn't go to plan. The USB stick was supposed to have been passed to Arthur via James. He was assured that James was careful, a trustworthy and reliable middleman, but then the damn thing had gone missing. James was young, a college kid who lived alone with his mother. No girlfriend, and didn't seem to have many friends. He was the perfect recruit, until this missing USB stick. There was nothing on the stick to connect it to Arthur, but none of them needed it getting into the wrong hands. Aside from the worry of it getting into the wrong hands, he had enjoyed the preview he received and had been looking forward to seeing the rest. Arthur had been in prison a long time and was impressed at the quality of images and filming today. The grainy content that had helped convict him was a thing of the past. You could even film on a mobile phone – this amazed Arthur. He smiled, feeling aroused.

Her

Her phone pinged a few times in quick succession. She glanced at the screen - it was the group WhatsApp chat. The details for Jenna's funeral had been announced. She confirmed she would be attending, took a deep breath and buried her face in her hands. When she looked back at her phone, there were 56 new messages. She sighed, scrolling through them, her heart beating as she read and took in the messages. The subject had moved on from Jenna to one of Jenna's cases, Arthur McIntyre, the paedo Head Teacher. This city really was small, and everyone was linked. It looked as though Dylan's mum had been one of his victims many years ago. No wonder the poor girl was so messed up. That didn't excuse her behaviour or the mess of a life she subjected that poor boy to, but it did give some understanding to the whole sorry story. What kinds of parents don't believe their daughter when she shares something like that with them? To trust them with something potentially so difficult and traumatic to share, and they stand back and watch as you subsequently go off the rails. And what kind of grandparents then go on to expose their grandson to the same predator? She'd have to give this some thought. What was the right approach? What was best for Dylan? The boy needs protecting. His grandparents failed to protect his mum, and they were now exposing him to the same threat. Instinct told her that the grandparents were the problem, but also, perhaps Arthur McIntyre would be a better candidate for her next act. It was clear that many people would be spared if he was banished from this life.

She filled her water spray, checking the soil of her lily of the valley before gently misting it as an idea took shape. She smiled. This time, she wanted to make a statement. People needed to know they couldn't get away with their behaviour. People abused their positions of power and good standing in the community far too often. This one needed to be made an example of.

Luke

The beat of the music made the floor vibrate, and the strobe lighting made everything look as though it was moving in slow motion. This was one of the few nightclubs that still displayed scantily clad dancers gyrating in cages suspended from the ceiling. Luke's gaze lingered on each cage as he looked around the room, before his eyes found Tilly, paying for a tray of shots. As he watched from afar, she picked up four shots in turn, downing each one. He saw her lean over the bar indicating to the barman as he pushed his way through the other clubbers to get to her.

'Tilly, I love you, babe, but you have got to slow down,' Luke frowned, watching Tilly swirl her straw in what he assumed was a vodka and lemonade. They were out with her friends. He gave them a look, but they just shrugged in return. As always, she was the life and soul of the party, suggesting more shots and dragging her friends to dance with her.

'I love this song,' she shouted over the music, spinning around. She stumbled slightly, before righting herself and stepping back towards Luke. Luke's face was fixed with a steely gaze. Her friends eyed her warily. 'When did you get so boring?' Tilly jabbed Luke in the chest, sneering at him when he would not be drawn into dancing with her.

'Around the same time, you turned into a drunk,' Luke retorted, immediately regretting it as he saw her eyes flash with hurt, quickly followed by anger. She turned from him to a man at the bar, asking if he wanted to buy her a drink. The man looked from Luke to Tilly and muttered that he had to be somewhere. Luke gave him a nod and a grateful smile as Tilly turned on him, accusing him of driving people away from her.

'Right, that's it, we're going home,' Luke said, grabbing Tilly and throwing her over his shoulder. She squealed, hammering on his back. As he left the bar and deposited her in a taxi, he asked a friend on the door to keep an eye on her friends and make sure they got into taxis safely.

The taxi driver turned in his seat 'she'd better not throw up back there,' he said, looking dubiously at Tilly, who had suddenly quietened down. Her body had lost its rigidity, and Luke noticed her eyelids drooping. She put her head on his shoulder. Luke glared at the driver and gave him the address.

'Just drive.'

'I don't deserve you,' she slurred, 'have I ever told you I don't deserve you? I don't deserve to be alive, not after what I did, and now Leanne is dead.' Luke hesitated, unsure where this was going. It was always the same whenever Tilly drank too much, which was often. She ranted about not being good enough for Luke and how he wouldn't love her if he knew what she had done, but this was the first time she had mentioned Leanne. As they got home, Tilly stumbled toward the sofa. Luke locked the door and sat beside her, giving her a gentle shake.

'It isn't time for sleep, Tilly. You were telling me a story. What happened with you and Leanne?'

'I killed her. It's my fault she is dead,' Tilly slurred matter-of-factly.

'You didn't kill her. Her drink was spiked,' Luke murmured.

'Yes. It was spiked by me. I did it. I killed my friend.' Her eyes closed as tiredness and alcohol took over.

Marie

Marie dropped her bag in the hallway, her wedding photo catching her eye. She paused for a moment, then took it down and slid it behind the hall table. She heard laughter from the living room and smiled. Her heart felt like it was swelling in her chest as she pushed open the living room door.

'I've missed you, my gorgeous, beautiful, adorable baby girls. I think you have both grown while I have been away. How was your weekend? Tell me everything,' gushed Marie pulling the girls into her arms and smothering them with theatrical kisses.

'You look well rested; the break must have done you good,' John smiled, leaning down to kiss her. John left the room to put the kettle on while Marie and the girls lined up on the sofa, gift bags in hand. The girls were quieter than usual, but Marie put it down to being tired or missing her.

'We went to the park and pretended to be famous, like on TV.'

'That sounds fun,' Marie said as she put her arms around them on the sofa next to her.

'We played dress up and John took our photos.'

Marie's stomach lurched. 'Go up to your room and open your presents, girls. I will be up in a minute.' Her heart raced as she went into the kitchen and shut the door.

'Who the fuck are you?' her eyes flashed, 'why the hell were you taking pictures of my children? Are you some kind of pervert who preys on vulnerable women?' John froze for a second, his back to Marie as she unleashed her sudden rage. He turned, having quickly regained his composure and stepped towards her, his arms widespread, palms facing her as if to embrace her. He grinned.

'Don't you come near me,' Marie yelled.

'You've got the wrong end of the stick. Think about what you are accusing me of. You know me. You know who I am. You're a good mother. After all you went through with Carl, you wouldn't let anyone bad into those girls' lives, you know you wouldn't.' Marie wavered for a minute. Sensing her resolve weaken, John took another step towards her.

'W-w-why else would you be taking photos of children?' she stuttered.

'I wasn't taking photos of children,' he said, 'I was taking photos of *your* children. As a surprise for you. I was going to get them framed for your birthday. If you think I'm capable of what you are suggesting, I think it best I leave now. Or perhaps you would like me to wait in the living room whilst you call the police? Clearly, you have decided I am some kind of monster. All I've ever done is be there for you and love you. And I love those girls as if they are my own.' John made a move towards the door, then paused for Marie's reply.

'Wait. Don't go.'

'I think it's best I do. I'll come by to get my things when we have both had some space.' John's voice was low and monotone as he left, closing the door silently behind him.

Marie stood still, staring at the door. It had all happened so quickly. One minute they were pleased to see each other, and the next, he was gone. She slipped her feet into her shoes and yanked open the door to follow him. She stopped as she heard the girls upstairs talking to each other. Maybe the space would be good, she mused, and he was right; she had accused him of being a paedophile. She laughed to herself. The idea seemed ridiculous now, even only a few minutes after it happened. He was her John, the man who had helped her and her girls through what could have been the worst time of their life. She suggested to the girls that they snuggle up on the sofa with ice cream and a DVD. When she was in the kitchen getting the supplies together, she sent a quick text to John, *I'm sorry, please forgive me.*

Marie pulled open the curtains, stifling a yawn. The sun was still rising, but she could not get back to sleep. She rubbed her eyes, looking at the clock on the bedside table. John would be awake by now, getting ready for work. Her bed had felt empty last night as she had spread her arms over the cold space beside her. Marie thought of the girls in the next room, her chest contracting. Everything was okay until Beth started asking questions about him. Bloody Social Workers were all the same, planting ideas in people's heads. It was as if they wanted to see people fail. She was being silly and paranoid. John didn't answer her first call, but she heard his gruff answer on the third attempt. Marie let out the breath she had been holding. She heard herself begging him to come back, heard herself apologising.

'I want you to get hold of your social worker and get her to do a background check to prove I've done nothing wrong.'

Marie sat down on the bed, her frown dissolving; he wouldn't be suggesting that if there was anything wrong. She agreed and resolved to ring Beth as soon as possible so they could put all this behind them.

The Professionals

'I need to be sure that you can safeguard Dylan from harm,' Beth said to Martha. Martha turned to Brian, looking anxious as she said they would never let any harm come to him. Brian put his arm around Martha, glaring protectively at Beth.

'What kind of people do you think we are?'

Beth sighed. She wasn't asking them to stop seeing Arthur but saying she had to be sure that Dylan was not at risk. She was frustrated by Martha and Brian, who were still taking Arthur's side over their own daughter's words all those years ago. Beth struggled to put aside her own maternal feelings. She would do everything within her power to love and protect her children. She couldn't imagine any circumstances where she wouldn't. Some days she had to work harder than others to separate work and personal feelings – this was one of those days. Beth was also concerned that Dylan might find out about the accusations his mum made towards Arthur. The boy had already been through enough - losing his mum and moving in with his grandparents. They agreed to give the situation some thought, and Beth would speak to them in a fortnight. Returning to the office, Beth sighed, leaning back in her desk chair, stretching her legs out under the desk in front of her.

She cast her eye over her 'to do' list, striking off another item as the dull vibrating of her phone ringing started up. Marie spoke fast, stumbling over her words.

'That was weird.' Beth said to her colleague as she got off the phone. 'Marie, the one with the cute twins, whose husband died on The Barbican a few months ago, just called. She's got a new boyfriend and wanted to ask if there is any way we can do background checks for her. Thing is, his ex-girlfriend recently reported that she felt something wasn't right when she was with him. Enough of a gut feeling for her to end the relationship with him. He doesn't have any kids of his own, but always seems to date single mums. Katie looked into it, and he had no previous, but something has got Marie questioning him.'

Beth rang Katie asking if she was free for a cuppa. 'I just want to have a bit of a catch-up on the Marie and John situation.'

'Sounds intriguing. See you later.' Katie rang off.

Katie waited for the computer to start up to check her ongoing cases before meeting Beth. She saw an email with the subject USB, frowning as she clicked on it. She was not prepared for the contents. The USB stick contained several indecent images of children. She had been asked to give a statement as to how this came to be in her possession. She was also tasked with getting a statement from Kylie. The USB drive was being checked for fingerprints. Katie leaned back in her chair, letting out a breath she hadn't realised she was holding. This was big. Where the hell had the stick come from? It had to be someone who attended Phoenix.

'Tom, want to head over to Phoenix with me? I'll fill you in on the way. This feels like something big.' Their communication had been frosty since Jenna's death, but all was now forgotten. Tom grabbed his keys. By the time they had taken Kylie's statement and requested the sign-in register for everyone in the building the day she received the USB stick, they had been urgently summoned back to the station to attend a task force meeting for the investigation, now named Operation Delamere.

~

Jenna's funeral was tough for everyone. The crematorium was small, and the limited seating filled quickly. People were left standing at the back and in the foyer. Jenna had been well-liked by colleagues and offenders, and the service was a time when those on both sides of the law were able to come together in mourning. At the wake, people split off into the usual cliques of family, friends and colleagues. Beth, Emma, Kylie and Anna sat together at the social club.

Grace was at the bar when she heard Anna cry out, 'What the fuck?' She stuffed her change in her purse and hurried back with the tray of drinks in time to hear Beth filling them in on Marie's request for a background check on John.

'I am sick of stupid bloody women not putting their kids first and men thinking with their dicks,' said Anna, slurring her words slightly. Her voice cracked as she continued speaking. 'None of us would be here if Tom had managed to keep it in his pants and hadn't been such an arse. We all know that he pushed her over the edge.' The table fell quiet. Everyone knew and liked Tom, but they also saw how he treated women. He got away with it because he gave a wink and a smile; he charmed his way out of judgement, and most people that knew him had the good sense not to cross the friendship line. They exchanged uncomfortable looks at the uncharacteristic outburst from the usually calm and measured Anna. Ever the peacemaker, Beth jumped in to point out that it wasn't just

Tom. They all knew Jenna had her own demons before Tom came on the scene. 'The demons didn't get her pregnant and then abandon her.' Anna downed her drink and walked out, Grace scurrying after her.

Bernie

Bernie sat upright in the chair, her hands clenched in front of her. The room was small and she looked around, in vain, for a window to open. She had been hauled into the police station for a formal interview. Her fingerprints had been found on the USB stick. She was out of her depth and didn't know what to say.

'I- I found it. I don't trust police,' she looked down, trying to conceal the tremors, attempting to keep her voice light. She picked at her nail varnish. 'I left it for Kylie as I knew she would know what to do. What is on it?'

'You don't need to concern yourself with that. We just need to know where it came from. For your own sake, you need to start telling us the truth.'

Bernie went home after the interview, locked the door and sat lost in thought. Her phone rang. She ignored it. It rang again. Shit. She was supposed to be cleaning today. She couldn't go - how could she go there? There was obviously something terrible on that USB stick. She couldn't face Jackie, let alone risk bumping into James. She tapped out a text message to Jackie, *so sorry, can't make it today - not well, might be catching - will call soon to rearrange.* Bernie switched her phone off and threw it down beside her. Then frowned, and turned it back on again, remembering the police said to keep her phone on as they may need to contact her again. Deep down, she knew she had to do the right thing and tell the police that it was James, but what would happen to her if she did? Bernie's stomach was doing somersaults. She had felt the wrath of Luke when she crossed him before. Grassing to the police was an inexcusable sin in their world, let alone grassing up his brother. But then, she didn't know what he had done, and she knew deep down it was probably much, much worse than being a grass.

The
Professionals

The group room was filled with new faces, their body language giving away their barely concealed nerves - twitching knees or fiddling with bracelets or watches. This was their first chance to establish their place in the group. Some people had a more confident stance, leaning back, legs akimbo, holding eye contact with anyone who looked their way.

The latest addiction group was about to start. The first session was always interesting - first impressions were forming. Tom knew his uniform meant he had to work harder to build trust and a rapport than the other staff. The different agencies were always represented on day one, so Tom was joined by Grace, Sally and Kylie. There was also a worker from the Housing Association to give out some leaflets and offer support. Tom relished being the only man. He enjoyed seeing the way Sally and the Housing Worker hung on to his every word. He winked at Sally, who blushed and looked down. Tom surveyed the group members. They were the same as always. Every time a group started, they had different names and faces, but their stories didn't vary much - The drink drivers with an air of superiority who didn't feel they fitted in with the real criminals. Then, there were the wife beaters with the usual tale of woe - *my wife doesn't understand me.* The bored housewives who drank to fill the lonely void - *my husband is never home.* The usual mix of drug addicts and drinkers, mostly homeless or sofa surfing with stereotypical tales of turbulent relationships and abusive upbringings. Generally, the recurring theme of the group was blame – who can I blame for the situation I am in now? Round and round we go, thought Tom.

~

Beth spotted Katie coming out of the meeting room and made a beeline for her. 'Any chance you are free to visit Marie with me later? I still can't crack her, to get her to open up fully. Perhaps with a different dynamic, she might open up a bit more.'

'You're in luck. I have a couple of statements I need to take, but can come by with you at the end of the day, say 5 pm, if that's not too late?'

'I'll meet you there,' Beth nodded. She gave Marie a quick call to let her know.

Beth waited by her car until Katie pulled up. John answered the door to them, and they exchanged a look. 'We may need to take some details from you, but for now, we need to meet with Marie on her own,' Beth explained. Marie suggested he take the girls to the park. Katie and Beth sat side by side on the old sofa. Marie remained standing, watching John and the children out of the window as they left. Beth cleared her throat, and Marie eventually took a seat in the armchair.

'I don't know what I was thinking. Silly really. Just got in my own head. I am so sorry to have troubled you, Beth, and wasted your time'. She directed the last bit at Katie.

Katie and Beth tried to encourage her to think back to anything specific that may have triggered her anxiety. Marie

256

mentioned the photos John took while she was away, quickly jumping to defend John when she saw Katie frown.

'There is nothing in our records to indicate that John poses any immediate risk or threat to you or the girls,' Katie advised Marie, 'but that doesn't mean there is no risk as every situation has its own points to consider. Something made you call Beth, call it a gutting feeling or women's intuition, but just keep an eye on it and call us if you feel worried again.'

'It is better to ring and find nothing, than to ignore the warning signs until it's too late,' Beth finished. She left her final statement hanging in the air, before standing to indicate the meeting was over.

As they left, Katie and Beth passed John coming back to the house with the girls. Katie made eye contact with him and felt the sensation of the hairs on the nape of her neck standing on her, a cold shiver ran down her spine. She forced her mouth into a smile and turned to look at the girls. The smile froze. She recognised them. She recognised them from the USB stick. Katie's stomach lurched, and she fought the urge to stop and confront John. She kept walking until she had turned the corner, where she stopped and leaned on the wall, tiling her head back to rest on the hard stone. She couldn't share this with Beth yet. She needed to figure out what this meant.

'I'm not feeling too well, so I'm going to shoot straight off, but keep your phone on as I might need to get hold of you when I have checked something out,' she said as she got in the car, shutting the door and driving away before Beth could ask any questions.

As she drove back to the station, Katie called the police sergeant in charge of Operation Delamere and filled her in. An urgent meeting was being called. Katie arrived at the station and nodded at Tom as he joined her, making her way to the briefing room. Katie was asked to share what she had discussed with her superior. The biggest priority was safeguarding the children, so it was agreed they needed to be put on an immediate order for police protection. This would give them 72 hours to investigate further.

'I know Marie, and her social worker, Beth, so would like to be a part of the team that removes the children,' Katie volunteered. It wasn't a nice task to volunteer for, but Katie was always able to see beyond the unpleasantness of the situation and recognise when the humanity of a known face would make this marginally better for Marie. She was dispatched with colleagues to start the process while the meeting continued.

Marie

Less than an hour after Beth and Katie had left, Katie knocked on Marie's door again.

'I'll get it,' Marie shouted from the kitchen, up to John, who was bathing the girls. She turned off the hob and wiped her hands on a tea towel as she made her way to the front door. She saw blue lights through the opaque glass in the front door and felt her heart rate quicken as she opened it. Her mind jumped to her sister until she saw Beth and Katie standing on the doorstep with three uniformed officers behind them. None of them were smiling. The blood drained from Marie's face, and an icy chill ran down her spine. They explained the girls needed to be taken into protective custody immediately. John appeared at the top of the stairs. She saw his face and felt terror, the icy chill spreading like an iron vice, taking hold of her body. She tried to breathe, but no air reached her lungs. John's face was akin to that of a child caught with their hand in the biscuit tin. They were told they could go to the station voluntarily to assist with police enquiries, or if they refused, they would be arrested. Marie and John were led separately from the house and guided into the back seats of waiting police cars. Marie stared out of the window, seeing the shadow of her neighbour at the window. The girls, her girls, were being led out of the house, accompanied by Beth, who was carrying a holdall. The tears flowed silently down her cheeks, and she turned away as the car engine shuddered to life.

At the station, Marie and John were held in separate interview rooms. She was offered the chance to contact a solicitor but declined. Marie was alone in the room. The walls were bare, apart from a poster advertising The Samaritans. One wall had a large reflective window like those she had seen on TV. The chair was hard and uncomfortable. Marie couldn't remember if she had turned the hob off. The door opened, and an unfamiliar officer stepped in, again offering her a solicitor and reiterating the seriousness of the situation was in. She just wanted to be at home with her girls.

Marie was asked the same questions repeatedly. Was there anything she needed to tell them? Would it be easier for her in the long run if she told them everything now? What did she know about a USB stick? Eventually, after what felt like hours of questioning, Katie entered the room. Marie blew her cheeks out, relieved at finally seeing a familiar face. The relief was temporary, and her body stiffened as she remembered – all this happened after Katie's visit. She looked down, clenching her jaw, not trusting herself to speak. Katie finally gave her some information.

'We have reason to believe that your children are at immediate risk of being used to create indecent images. At this point, we also have reason to believe there may already be images in circulation. We have found several folders on a USB stick containing very serious images and videos of children. Not all the children are identifiable, but when I visited your home earlier, I recognised them from images I have seen as part of an ongoing investigation. Marie didn't understand it; there couldn't be, how could there be? Katie asked if there was anyone else who had care of the girls, anyone who might have taken indecent images.

Marie shook her head. 'No, no. There is no-one. It can't be my girls'.

Katie stared at her.

Marie pictured John's face at the top of the stairs when the police came, and the bile rose up in her throat. She swallowed. She recalled what the girls had said after John had sent her away for the weekend with her sister, *we played dress up and had our photos taken*. Marie shakily recounted the conversation to Katie and her colleague.

'What has he done to my girls?'

Katie recommended she speak with a duty solicitor. This time, Marie agreed.

Her

It was easy to plan a time to get Arthur alone. He was often in his shed on the allotment. She had been watching his routine. She saw him leave the house carrying golf clubs in that ridiculous attire golfers seem to gad about in. Sometimes she followed him to the Golf and Country Club, others, he veered off to the allotment.

The allotment itself had many plots mapped out, and was on a big flat piece of land with one edge bordering a main road. The car park was accessed through a residential area on the other side. She parked a couple of streets away and saw only Arthur's car in the car park. There were no other cars. She'd been here a few days ago with a gas bottle she positioned behind Arthur's shed and covered by propping a few old bits of wood she found lying around up against it. She piped the end into the shed through a small hole. The wooden shed wasn't airtight, but hopefully, the gas would do its job. She'd planned this one and felt better for it.

Arthur made his way across the allotments, and she followed at a safe distance, keeping cover behind hedges and sheds. He glanced around before unlocking his padlock and slipping inside. She moved closer and crouched with her trowel over someone's flower bed. It was silent except for the rumble of cars in the distance. She looked at her watch. He had been in the shed for a few minutes. She crept closer and paused behind the shed, listening. She reached behind the planks of wood and turned the tap on the gas canister, catching her breath at the almost imperceptible hiss of the gas leaving the bottle. She looked around. The allotment was still empty. Her heart was thumping in her chest, her senses heightened. She remained motionless, checking her watch again. It was still silent. Three minutes had passed. She crept to the side of the shed, pausing. Her hand closed around the cool metal of the padlock in her pocket. Could he hear her heart beating? Five minutes! She rose from her position and closed the well-oiled latch on the door, silently slipping the padlock through the hook. She moved away and dropped to crouch by a herb garden. As he coughed inside the shed, she breathed in the scent of Rosemary. A car pulled into the car park. Her pulse quickened. She watched. Waited. The car remained stationary. Nine minutes. The car pulled away. Arthur's coughing was constant now. She heard the thud of his palm on the door. There was a grunt and another thud as the door shook.

'Hello? HELLO. Is there anybody there?'

11 minutes. She waited, rubbing the rosemary between her gloved hands and inhaling the woody scent. The hammering on the door had intensified for a few moments before gradually growing weaker. She looked at her watch, waiting for a full minute of silence to pass before closing the distance between her and the door. She risked peering through a crack and saw him slumped on the floor.

She switched off the gas, pulling up a bandana from around her neck. Her nose and mouth covered, she stepped inside, pulling the door shut behind her. She took the school tie from her pocket, running the soft silk through her fingers, smiling. He had fallen on his side, and she manoeuvred herself behind him, pushing him forward so she could loop the tie around his neck in a noose. The shed was warm, and she felt her scalp prickling. The bandana stopped her from getting a deep breath, protecting her from the gas. She braced her foot against his back whilst she increased the pressure of the noose on his windpipe. She let his body sink to the floor, a dead weight, and burst out of the shed, ripping the bandana off and breathing in the fresh air. She sank down, dizzy from the fumes, leaning against the shed, breathing slowly.

She went back in. She left the tie looped around his neck and surveyed his prone body. His belt was already unbuckled. She turned her head away and tugged his trousers and white pants down, panting with the exertion. As they moved freely down his calves, she turned back and stopped for a moment, suppressing the urge to giggle at the old man's bottom. She took a deep breath in and pushed him over and up into a sitting position, wincing as she caught sight of his shrivelled old balls.

She looked around for the first time and saw his hiding place exposed. She shuddered at the feel of being in the viper's nest. There were various mobile phones, a laptop and a couple of USB sticks. There was also a notebook. She hesitated; her brow furrowed. What if someone in on it found him, and they got rid of the evidence? She could take it and plant it in his house or his car. She looked over the stash again, selecting one of the USB sticks in case she needed it. Checking her watch, she looked around for signs that she had been there before slipping out of the shed. She took care to leave the door ajar. Grabbing the gas canister, she made her way back to the car, ready to dispose of it on the way home, along with her shoes and gloves. She turned the radio on and smiled as she heard Lizzo singing It's about damn time.

Luke

Luke didn't know what to do. Tilly was drinking more and more and refusing to talk about what she had revealed. She spent all her time at his place now, refusing to go home or speak to her mum. Luke tried to get her to talk to her parents. Much as he hated so many things her wealthy family stood for, he also understood the importance of family. His thumb hovered over her mum's number in Tilly's phone, unsure what to do. He had left Tilly sleeping off another hangover and went to see his mum to get her opinion.

'Oh, love,' said Jackie. She knew he was in an impossible position - tell Tilly's parents and risk Tilly hating him, or not tell them and risk this spiralling even more. Either way, it would not improve their opinion of him. Luke eventually made the difficult decision that he would have to tell them. Sometimes, you had to go against the grain. He just wanted her to be okay. Christ, when had he become such a sentimental push over? Once the decision was made, he took Tilly's phone and rang her dad, arranging to meet up. Her dad told him to come to the house the following evening. Luke was undecided if he should have the conversation with them on his own first, or if he should bring Tilly so it was all out in the open.

~

'How could you?' Tilly yelled at Luke. Her dad had phoned her to ask if she knew what Luke wanted to talk to him about. Luke ducked as she threw her phone at him, followed by a cushion, a remote control and a series of other objects within her reach.

'You are just as bad as they are, trying to control my life,' she screamed, refusing to hear any reasoning from Luke. He couldn't deal with her when she was like this. He tried, but left, deciding to get some air and walk to her parent's house. The evening air was cool, and the walk gave him a chance to think about the conversation he planned to have with them. Luke loved Tilly, and she was the first good thing in his life that had made him want to change and be a better person. He finally felt a reason to get out of this life that was all he had known and go straight. He knew he didn't deserve that after some things he had done and wasn't proud of, but was glad he had this second chance to get things right. He just had to get her parents on side so they could all come up with a plan to help get Tilly back on track.

Tilly's parents reluctantly greeted him and showed him to the conservatory. He looked around at the spacious, airy room with its light furniture and trailing plants. He wasn't offered a drink.

'I am sure Tilly will be along soon, so we can all hear what you have to say,' Tilly's dad said, looking at his watch. The doorbell chimed. 'Aha,' he said with a smug glance towards Luke as he left the room.

Luke looked at his phone, seeing a missed call from Tilly and a voicemail message. He heard Tilly's dad shouting for her mum, so pressed play while he waited for them. Tilly was shouting in the message, her voice slurry and abrasive, as he heard she said she was on her way. She continued to rant explicitly as the revving of a car engine drowned out some of her words. The line went dead.

Bernie

Bernie took the milk from Jackie, adding it to the mugs of tea. She took her time straining the tea bags and took a deep breath before turning and putting the mugs on the kitchen table.

'Is everything okay? You don't seem yourself,' Jackie raised her eyebrows at Bernie.

'I may need to go away for a while. I came by this evening to let you know how much I have appreciated the job, but more than that, our friendship. And I wanted to say goodbye.'

'Whatever's happened, we can sort it.' Jackie put her hand over Bernie's. 'Are you in some kind of trouble? Is it money? I'll call Luke?'

'No! Don't call Luke! There is nothing that will fix this. It's just something that I have to do.'

Bernie knew she had to tell the police where the USB stick came from and face the consequences. She knew she could be arrested for withholding information. She also knew how easy it would be for other people to make her disappear when they found out what she had done. Perhaps she would run if, by some miracle, they didn't arrest her.

She saw the girls down at Docker Street on the way to the station and fought back tears as she hugged them goodbye. She never had children, but some of the girls were young enough to be her daughters and looked to the older woman for a mother figure.

'Look after yourselves, girls, and I will be back.'

She passed Tom as she walked away from her girls. He was in plain clothes and appeared to be there on off-duty business. She gave him a nod, put her head down and kept walking. She walked through the city centre, her decision weighing heavily in her heart, which was beating faster than usual. The thudding vibrated as if it was trying to escape her body. She took a deep breath and ignored the butterflies in her stomach as she walked through the doors of Charles Cross Police Station.

'I have some information I need to share about an ongoing case.'

'If you take a seat, someone will be along when they can.' The monotone desk sergeant barely looked up.

Bernie checked the clock for the umpteenth time, jiggling her knee. The waiting room was windowless, and there was little airflow. She pulled her cigarettes from her bag and stood up just as she heard a voice ask how they could help.

'It is probably nothing, but I just wanted to speak to you about a USB stick I found.'

Bernie was ushered into an interview room. She looked around. It was nicer than the interview rooms she had previously been in. This time, she had been shown to the interview room reserved for witnesses and members of the general public, rather than the bleak room you were taken to when you were arrested or under suspicion. The chairs were cushioned, and there was a large green leafy plant in the corner of the room. Bernie told the detectives all she knew. She told them she felt something wasn't right with James, that there was something dark about him. She told them about the porn, the conversation on the phone outside and, most importantly, that she got the USB stick from him. She told them she hadn't known what to do, so hoped if she left it for Kylie, it would get looked at. She said she knew once she was called in, she should have said where she got it from, but she was scared. The detectives thanked her and left the room, saying they would be back. The desk sergeant brought in a fresh jug of water and put it on the table in front of her.

When the detectives returned, they said they had come to speak to her about her safety. The matter of withholding information and potentially perverting the cause of justice would be dealt with as a separate matter, but right now, they needed to ensure she was safe. They asked if she was prepared to testify what she had told them in court. Bernie hesitated, then nodded and whispered that she would. The detectives said they felt there was justification for putting her in temporary witness protection whilst the investigation was ongoing for her own safety.

'What? I can't just...'

'It would be for your own safety, just while the case is ongoing.'

Bernie nodded. Once she had agreed, everything seemed to happen quickly, and she was taken through to a different part of the station, where she was told to wait while arrangements were made.

'What about my methadone script? My flat? My clothes, I need my clothes.'

'All of this will be sorted out. Our priority is your safety, and we think it is important to keep you in immediate protective custody until we can get everything in place. Tell you what, why don't I get you a notebook and pen, and you can start making a note of any questions you have.'

The
Professionals

Operation Delamere was a big case, and reporters were calling the police press office for updates. A few waited outside the station, asking officers for information at every opportunity. There had been bits of information printed, but so far, no names or specifics had been leaked. James was in custody following the information from Bernie. A search warrant had turned up nothing except a burner phone hidden in a plant pot, so far. The phone had been used but wiped, so it was going to take time for the tech team to retrieve the data. They had phone numbers from the call log but no one to link the numbers to. They could only hold James for 24 hours but were confident in a court application to keep him for longer.

~

Katie had an update from Beth that Marie's children were okay. They had already been through a lot in their short lives, seen more than children should see, and were developing a level of emotional resilience that they shouldn't have had to develop. Katie didn't know if it was sadder if kids struggled to cope when being taken away or sadder if they didn't. There was still the matter of identifying the other children in the images and figuring out what the girls had been through. There was a long journey ahead of them. Marie and John had both been released pending further investigation and told they needed to keep police informed of their whereabouts. Search warrants had been issued, and their homes and cars had been searched, with all electronic devices being removed. They were forbidden from contacting each other.

So, was it him? Her? Or were they both in on it? asked Anna in the WhatsApp group. The girls had had little chance to meet up with the big investigation going on. It impacted all of them in one way or another. Katie couldn't share much, but she and Beth both agreed it looked like it was all down to John, and that Marie hadn't known. Sally said she couldn't believe that Marie didn't have some idea, *how you could let a monster into your bed and not know?* Emma merely replied to comments with a *WTF* or *FFS*. On the subject of paedophiles, they shared that Arthur hadn't attended his latest appointment, and no one had heard anything of him. They all agreed he had been flying under the radar of late, *makes you wonder if he is tied up in all this Operation Delamere business somehow,* Grace speculated.

~

Tom's phone rang, and he saw it was the cute housing worker that had given a talk at the addiction group recently. He smiled, answering it with a flirtatious tone.

'Clearly, you didn't get enough of me at Phoenix.' His tone quickly changed when he heard what she had to say. She had just had two of her rough sleepers in for an appointment. They said they had been sleeping at local allotments. They had smelled a funny smell but assumed it was just some sort of weed killer or garden chemical. When they eventually

272

investigated, they found a body. They didn't know what to do and didn't want to be accused of anything, so they had shut the shed door and left. This was last night, and they had panicked this morning, coming into the office, not sure what to do. Tom let her know they would need to speak to her and her clients properly, and he would get officers down there immediately. Tom radioed it in, and the nearest officers were dispatched to the allotment with an ETA of five minutes. All available units were on standby. Tom mused that it was probably a false alarm, a pair of homeless junkies getting confused, but followed it up with urgency, just in case.

Her

It took longer than she expected, but it was all over the news within hours of him being found. He was too well known for the press not to have got hold of his name. They had enough police officers moonlighting on their newspaper's payroll to guarantee they got their story. Arthur's death was being investigated as a potential revenge attack by one of his many victims. She was proud of how this one was turning out. The news outlets had reported that police found laptops and mobile phones containing indecent images and videos. They found a notebook containing bank account information and personal details for those involved in the distribution. It seems Arthur may have adapted to modern technology in some ways but not well enough to have covered his tracks. He clearly wasn't at the top of this outfit, but they had linked him to James, John and a few others involved in the ring. Thanks to Arthur's old school, and meticulous record keeping, they had everything they needed to build a good case and put people away for a long time.

She heard Bernie had been taken into Witness Protection. She hoped Bernie would stay strong as her evidence would hopefully help to build the case and make sure James was put away for a long time. Long enough for her to plan his fate on release, anyway. She was proud of what she had achieved with

Arthur. She felt she had a part to play in the arrests – the police would never have got there without her using Arthur's body to guide them to the evidence.

Her project this evening was significantly less arduous than the despatch of Arthur. She had added a generous dose of sleeping pills to the whiskey of her next victim while he was away. Today, he was home. Tonight, she would pay him a visit. The streets were dark, inky shadows stretching across the roads. It was a long run, but she didn't want to use her car with so little traffic on the roads. She enjoyed the peacefulness of making her way through the city at night; the houses shrouded in darkness. Every building became a mystery, looming in the shadows. She reached her destination and scanned the windows, seeing nothing to indicate he was still awake. During her last visit, she had pocketed his spare key for ease of access tonight. The door opened silently and she crept to the kitchen, reaching out a gloved hand to turn the gas on. As the familiar hissing sound began, she took the whiskey bottle and the empty glass beside it and saw herself out, locking the door behind her.

It was not long until the big move. She loved Plymouth, and had so many memories, but it was time to move on. The house was mostly packed, and her new property would be waiting for her in a few weeks. She had a nice long holiday booked in between to recharge her batteries. There were a few loose ends to tie up, and she would be in a new city for a fresh start.

Luke

Tilly was in hospital.

She had taken Luke's car keys and attempted to drive to her parents. She was well over the drink drive limit, and without insurance or a licence. Luke's car was a write-off. Tilly had been unconscious for a few days – they kept her sedated to manage the pain. Luckily, no one else had been involved in the accident, but the engine caught alight, and Tilly was badly burned.

When Tilly woke, she asked her parents to tell Luke she never wanted to see him again. She would have lasting burn scars and would need a long period of physiotherapy and rehabilitation. Luke could still sense her presence at home. The blanket on the back of the sofa still had the faint aroma of her perfume. There was a note on the fridge, and his stomach lurched every time he went to the fridge and saw her handwriting - the little heart over her i's - he imagined her smiling as she wrote it. The paper was crumpled where he screwed it up to stop looking at it. He fished it out of the bin an hour later, smoothing it out on the worksurface and sticking it back on the fridge.

If only he could go back in time, he wouldn't have left her during the argument. He wouldn't have spoken to her parents. He wouldn't have let her drinking get so bad. He should have looked after her. Luke knew she meant it when she said she didn't want to see him again. With James on remand, it was just Luke and Jackie now. Luke had some big decisions to make – many people didn't want to work for, or do business for a nonce's brother. Luke felt the bile rising up in his throat every time he thought about what his brother had been charged with. His mother begged him to get James the best lawyer to get him home and then they could get him help. Luke couldn't forgive that easily. He had to make his stance on his brother clear and show the people he worked with that he was as disgusted by his brother as the rest of the world. How could he do that without hurting the person he loved most in the world? The only person he had left.

Marie

Marie didn't recognise the officer who delivered the news to her. John was killed in a gas leak a few days after the police had released him. He would never get to face the charges and answer to the evidence they had against him. They were still waiting for investigators to determine the cause of the gas leak. The police had always been nice to her in the past when Carl was alive. Since her arrest, the sympathetic smiles and offers of support were gone. Words were used sparingly, and eye contact was rare. If they did bother to make eye contact, it was prolonged and piercing, as if they were staring into her soul, forcing her to look away. She had been cleared of any wrongdoing, but they still spoke to her as if she was the one in the wrong - as if she was the paedophile.

The girls had been spoken to by specially trained staff who said there was nothing to indicate any physical harm had taken place. Marie had been given contact information for child trauma counselling and support groups.

Whilst the girls were in temporary foster care, Marie had been allowed supervised visits. Her heart felt like it was breaking in two, seeing them in the foster home. They smiled and played and ran around as if it was their home. Beth encouraged her to try to see some positives in this, observing what adaptable and resilient little girls they are.

'They should be back with you by the end of the week, but we will need to meet again. The girls need to be your priority now.' Beth looked at Marie pointedly. Marie wept with tears of happiness. She swore she would never look at another man again.

Marie lay in bed thinking back over her life, the choices she had made to bring her to this point. She wept until her swollen eyes had no more tears to cry.

Dylan

Dylan knew something serious was going on when his grandparents sat him down and said they had something they needed to tell him. They began by speaking about their friend Arthur, and his recent death. Brian took Martha's hand, and they told Dylan everything. They told him about his mum and what she had accused Arthur of. They told him how they hadn't believed her, and she had subsequently made many poor decisions and not very nice friends, leading to them no longer speaking to her.

'We can't keep secrets anymore; it isn't good for anyone,' Martha sobbed. Dylan heard how Arthur had gone to prison, and they had stuck by him, not believing what he had done. 'When all the accusations came out that got him sent to prison, we thought it was petty revenge. It was mostly people from council estates, tearaways out to cause trouble. We believed him. We thought they were making up stories as an excuse for messing their lives up.'

Brian and Martha told Dylan how, since his release, it looked like Arthur had been 'up to no good', and after his death, there was a lot of evidence found against him. Dylan didn't say a word as they spoke, alternating between them as they told the story. 'We understand if you don't want to live with us anymore, but we love you so, so much and want you to give us a second chance.' Dylan still said nothing.

'Well, Son? What have you got to say?'

'It's your fault my mum is dead. And I'm not your son.' Dylan whispered. He launched himself at his grandfather, punching and kicking him in a feral attack. Brian allowed him to continue whilst Martha sobbed. Eventually, Dylan stopped and crumpled to the floor, crying. Martha moved to him and gently put her arms around him, her grip tightening once she had him in her arms.

As a family, there was a sense of understanding. There were no more secrets. The damage had been done, but they would try to mend.

'Our Janie would have been proud of how you have dealt with everything. She loved you more than anything,' said Brian holding back his own tears of sadness.

Her

It was her last addiction group, and this was the last time she was guaranteed to see him. She couldn't risk phoning or emailing him. She had come too far for this womanising piece of shit to be her downfall. The group went well, and she made small talk with Tom as they headed back to the office. When they were alone in the corridor, she made her move.

'Fancy a drink after work one night?' She smiled at him, and his eyes lit up. She knew he would accept. Her whole professional world was based around believing that people can change and helping to guide that rehabilitation. Unfortunately, it was rare that she ever saw this happen. That is why they all had to go. She gave them so many chances, so many opportunities to stop being such fuck ups and hurting others. She didn't want them to prove her right, but they just kept doing it, time and time again. She knew not everyone would understand her actions. Some might say she was a cold killer, emotionless even. She wasn't cold; she didn't take joy from killing those people, well, not all of them. She was just doing society a favour, doing the world a favour. This was about making the world a better place.

She knew Tom would accept the drink invitation because he was just like the others; he hadn't changed, and he never would. He didn't see it as a platonic drink invitation; he saw it as a chance to fool around. Again. This was exactly what she was counting on. She knew the perfect spot for her last act of requital.

'Meet me at Cadover Bridge. Take the track up towards the quarry, and I will meet you in the last car park. It will be nice and quiet; we can walk up near the quarry, where we can get to know each other without interruption.' She held his gaze and let his imagination run wild.

Tom

There was something about her that seemed off. She appeared more energised than when he saw her at work, her eyes were shining, and she seemed almost skittish. It made her even more attractive to him, vixen-like. She was usually so poised and calm, but there was a strange energy in the air. He shook off the sense of unease, focusing on her pert bum leading the way along the path in front of him. She wore denim hot pants and boots, her long tanned legs displayed ahead of him. He had never seen her dressed so provocatively. She glanced over her shoulder to check he was keeping up and took a bottle of water from her bag, handing it to him with a smile that showed her teeth. His fingers brushed hers as he took it. It was a warm day, and he gulped it down gratefully.

'Drink as much as you want,' she said, 'I've got more in my bag.' He knocked back more of the cool liquid, putting the bottle in his back pocket and picking up his pace to keep up with her. They stopped to admire the view. He looked out across the moorland, his gaze panning to her standing beside him. She was The Unattainable, the one woman who was immune to his charms. Even Katie had a crush on him when they first met – she denied it, but he could always tell when women were into him. They all had the same tells – playing with their hair and giggling, they were asking for it. He had to lie to his wife and say he had been asked to stay late at work tonight, but it would be worth it. Just wait until the lads at the station heard about this.

'It's nice to get away from the city,' he said. 'Work has been pretty depressing the last few months - It feels like there has been one death after another to deal with. If I didn't know better, I'd say there was someone out there killing off our regulars.'

'How do you know there isn't?' she asked with an expressionless face, holding his gaze. 'Your face!' she laughed, putting her hand on his arm. His focus shifted to the warmth of her touch, reminding him what he was there for.

Tom's heart rate began to speed and his limbs were heavy. The air was thick with humidity, the kind of air that came before a storm, so he assumed the heat was getting to him. He pulled the bottle from his back pocket and drained the last of the water. He stumbled a little as he ducked under a branch and saw the grassy clearing ahead of them. It was like a private oasis surrounded on three sides by trees and gorse bushes. They were on the edge of the old quarry, and there were pretty views stretching out ahead of them, the yellow flowers on the gorse bushes were highlighted by the evening sun. He really didn't feel well now, but was determined to make the most of this chance.

'Have you ever considered being faithful, Tom?' He looked at her, shaking his head, thinking he had misheard. 'Men like you are all the same, you know, you have it all, a gorgeous wife and baby, a decent job and a house, and you always want more.' His skin prickled with unease again; this wasn't what he was expecting. 'Imagine if you were right with what you said before?'

'What do you mean?' he was slurring his words now, and his voice didn't sound right when he heard himself speaking.

'What you said about someone bumping off our regulars.' She used air quotes when she said bumping off. 'What did you think this little rendezvous was about? Did you really think I would be interested in a cheating shithead like you?'

Tom didn't want to listen anymore; he clenched his jaw, the vein in his forehead twitching. Were there people watching? Was this a joke? Someone he had screwed and not called back, trying to get revenge? His brain was foggy, and he tried to look around. His head was heavy, a dead weight on his shoulders. He remembered reading once that the average human head weighed 5kg. Tom saw the trees moving in slow motion as he turned his heavy head, and she came into his view. Her face reminded him he came here with a purpose. He needed to focus. He imagined them kissing as he leaned towards her. She moved away from him, and he felt his face hit the coarse dry grass.

'Come on Tom, you must realise now? Putting the pieces together? You are a copper, after all.' He looked at her face. She looked like a different person. Her eyes were cold, and a chill ran through him with the realisation that he had been drugged. His hand moved to the water bottle in his pocket. 'It was all me.' Her voice was different, far away. He didn't know if it was the drugs or her.

Her

'You had to be my last project before I leave,' she said to him. I was saving you. 'Your wife and daughter deserve better. The women of Plymouth deserve better than to have a predator like you leading them on and breaking their hearts. Do you have any idea how hard it has been, holding my tongue? Having to work with you day in, day out? You had so many chances to stop the cheating, to put your family first for a change, but you just kept at it. If I don't stop you now, you will ruin more lives. Of course, you are not my first. Carl was the first. He wasn't unlike you; do you remember him? He made his poor wife's life a misery. Turned out she was too stupid to be worth saving when she shacked up with a nonce. I get rid of one problem for her, and she goes straight out and creates another one.' She let out a deep breath, looking up. Finally. Someone she could confide in. She could almost see the tension leaving her body, allowing her to focus on her good deeds, not having to use her energy holding it all in.

'As for all the junkies, I did society a favour. Fiona did have some good points, to be fair to her, but she also had so many chances to change and didn't take them. Dylan's mum - I think most people would agree I did him a favour getting rid of her. I know she had a crappy time of it, but I sorted out a bit of payback for her in the end. Yes, old Arthur was some of my finest work. I am sure she would have been glad to see him off the street and despatched off once and for all. And her boyfriend Frank would only have ended up back inside, eventually. His poor old mum deserved to finally get a break from his selfish behaviour. Can you imagine, you have one son, your pride and joy, and he ends up killing two girls? Then on top of that, he learns nothing from prison and comes out, reigniting his alcoholism even worse than before. The poisoned flap jacks were a bit of a punt, it was messy. I need to get better at the poison because that could have been a beaut if I pulled it off. I know, I know, don't beat myself up, a couple did die, but I could have done better.'

Tom's eyes widened; his eyebrows shot up as she spoke. She didn't notice. Her voice had become singsong-like, melodic as she reminisced. 'That paedophile ring fell into my hands. It was planning the end of Arthur's story that made me realise I needed to start thinking things through a bit more. I wanted his death to have some meaning behind it, a link to his wrongdoings. I think I achieved that, don't you agree? Also, the naked bollocks and the school tie helped me stay under the radar as you and your pals were looking for a vengeful victim. The art of misdirection.' She paused in her monologue, smirking. 'I enjoyed the planning. Murder has some real scope to become an art form, don't you think? Anyway, those old pals of his were going to be next, Martha and Brian, but I think the kid probably just needed some stability, so I let them off. Hopefully, they have learned their lesson and don't have any other paedophiles on their Christmas card list. Although, do we ever really know who we are socialising with? Wait. Don't answer that. It seems an unfair question, given your current predicament.'

Tom

Tom's last thoughts as he let his body give in to the drugs were of his wife. His lovely, lovely wife. He pictured her laughing and smiling on their wedding day. Her face when she held their daughter for the first time quickly replaced by the pain on her face when she found out he had been unfaithful. He squeezed his eyes shut; his fist clenched. It was too late. He felt someone rummaging through his pockets and heard a distant voice asking if he had any last words. He opened his mouth and tried to speak. His tongue was in the way, and all that came out was a series of grunts and groans. He felt his thumb being pushed against a smooth surface as she used it to unlock his phone. He tried to open his eyes. His eyelids were heavy, and through the narrow slit, he saw a gloved hand holding his phone, tapping away.

'At least you left a note before you killed yourself,' she said, 'Do you want to know what you said?' She didn't wait for an answer. 'You emailed your work email address saying that you are sorry you haven't been the husband and father you should have been and that they are better off without you.' He felt his phone being roughly pushed back into a pocket. His eyes were too heavy to keep open as he stopped fighting and let them close. His body felt like it was moving, a rolling motion. He heard her huffing with exertion as she rolled his body, now a dead weight. His terror grew as he realised she was pushing him towards the edge of the quarry. The last thing Tom felt before the sensation of free falling was the warmth of urine spreading across his trousers, and then, nothing.

Her

She looked around for any signs of their presence. Before rolling Tom into the quarry, she had retrieved the water bottle from his pocket and put it in her bag, together with the gloves. Glancing over the edge, she could just about see where his body had broken through the bushes and branches before landing on the rocks at the bottom. There was no one else around, and it would hopefully be a few days before he was found. She would be long gone and far away by then. It would be a few hours before his wife started trying to call him. Given his past behaviour, no one would take his being AWOL seriously at first – they would assume he was off with a woman. Some of his colleagues may even try to cover for him. Even if he had told anyone he was meeting her, she had left her phone at home so she could not be tied to being in the area if anyone looked into it. Her car was parked a few miles away, so even if her car was seen on any cameras, she hopefully wouldn't be linked. She had thought of everything. If all went to plan, it would be deemed a suicide, anyway. She got away with the others, so this one shouldn't be any different.

Before reaching the main car park, she tucked behind a bush and changed into long jogging bottoms, pulling her hair into a low ponytail and putting on her baseball cap. She put her head down and marched back across the moor to her car. She had dinner plans to get back for. She let herself into the house and looked around her nearly empty home. Most of her belongings were in storage now. When she returned from her holiday, she planned to stay in a B&B until she was able to move into the next place she would call home. She ordered a selection of pizzas to arrive in an hour or so, and the girls were due any minute. This was her last goodbye. It would also give them all a good alibi in case it was needed. Much as she sometimes despaired of women for their stupid mistakes and poor taste in men, she had become quite fond of her colleagues. A couple of hours later, the pizza was being washed down with gin and bottles of beer. They were putting the world to rights when Katie's phone rang. It was Tom's wife.

'Is he with you? He said he had to work late.'

'I am sure he will turn up soon.'

Emma said nothing. Beth and Kylie were too engrossed in conversation to notice.

The next morning, she cleaned up the boxes and bottles from the night before, putting them straight into the recycling bin, had a shower and put the last of her personal possessions in her case.

The past few months had been a learning curve. She had allowed a new side of her persona to evolve. She didn't want to quieten her inner voice anymore. She spent years keeping her beliefs inside, remaining professional and soldiering on. It was time for Anna to make her mark. There was much to be learned from her recent endeavours. Anna now saw that she had a craft worth perfecting. She wanted to use this talent? Hobby? Calling? Whatever it was, for the greater good, to rid the world of evil and make space for those who deserved it. She wasn't sure what adventures were waiting for her, but she was ready for whatever opportunities came her way.

With one last glance around, she picked up her lily and stepped through the front door, locking it for the final time.

Acknowledgements

This book has come together with the help of so many people, I can't possibly name them all, but let's give it a go. I asked my sister for advice with this and she suggested I go with 'to my darling sister for keeping me sane and for having beautiful babies.' All valid points.

To Steph, Heather and Millie, the first people I told when I decided to write this story – thank you for being the first ones to say go for it and to keep encouraging me all the way to publication.

To the first two readers, Katie and Jenny, for being the ones that encouraged me to keep going after reading what I now realise was a very questionable first draft!

Leanne and Karina - thank you for your help with some very specific procedural, medical and body related questions...

Kadie – who else could I text in the middle of the night with some very macabre questions about death? And who else could I drag along to *that* writing masterclass?

Erin, where do I begin? Even when I don't believe in myself, your belief in me is always unquestionably unwavering. Thank you for being you.

Huge thanks to my lovely Editor, Tracey – your guidance and patience have been invaluable in helping my ideas come to life.

Big shout out to Mike of IDG Prints and Tony of Citrus Headspace for help with all things creative. Thank you for being so patient with me!!

To all the other lovely friends and beta readers, thank you for all your advice and input. There are too many people who I have bounced ideas and random questions off to name, but you are so appreciated.

To Mum, Dad and those of you who have been incredibly patient when I haven't let you sneak a peak, let alone get your hands on it - I wanted you to have the finished version and nothing less.

Special thanks to the writing community - The South Hams Author Network have given endless words of support and practical advice. And Write Magic... would I have made it without you guys? I really don't know if I would. Thank you so much for the encouragement and comradery. I remember one dark and stormy weekend that I wrote for about 16 hours with Vikki, and Sam and the weekday evening gang have been my constants.

It turns out, I have a lot of gratitude to give, but my final thank-you, lovely reader, is you. Thank you for reading, and I hope you enjoyed reading 'Her' as mu ch as I enjoyed writing it.

Printed in Great Britain
by Amazon